The UnResolved

The UnResolved

T.K. WELSH

Dutton Books

DUTTON CHILDREN'S BOOKS

A division of Penguin Young Readers Group ✒ Published by the Penguin Group
Penguin Group (USA) Inc., 375 Hudson Street, New York, New York 10014, U.S.A.
Penguin Group (Canada), 90 Eglinton Avenue East, Suite 700, Toronto, Ontario, Canada
M4P 2Y3 (a division of Pearson Penguin Canada Inc.) ✒ Penguin Books Ltd, 80 Strand,
London WC2R 0RL, England ✒ Penguin Ireland, 25 St Stephen's Green, Dublin 2, Ireland
(a division of Penguin Books Ltd) ✒ Penguin Group (Australia), 250 Camberwell Road,
Camberwell, Victoria 3124, Australia (a division of Pearson Australia Group Pty Ltd) ✒
Penguin Books India Pvt Ltd, 11 Community Centre, Panchsheel Park, New Delhi - 110 017,
India ✒ Penguin Group (NZ), Cnr Airborne and Rosedale Roads, Albany, Auckland 1310,
New Zealand (a division of Pearson New Zealand Ltd) ✒ Penguin Books (South Africa) (Pty)
Ltd, 24 Sturdee Avenue, Rosebank, Johannesburg 2196, South Africa ✒
Penguin Books Ltd, Registered Offices: 80 Strand, London WC2R 0RL, England

Library of Congress Cataloging-in-Publication Data
Welsh, T. K.
The unresolved / T.K. Welsh.
p. cm.
Summary: In 1904 New York City, the spirit of a deceased German American teenage girl
searches for the person responsible for the Slocum steamboat fire that claimed her life and the
lives of more than 1000 other passengers.
ISBN 0-525-47731-4 (hardcover)
1. General Slocum (Steamboat)—Juvenile fiction. [1. General Slocum (Steamboat)—Fiction.
2. Fires—New York (State)—New York—Fiction. 3. Shipwrecks—Fiction. 4. Ghosts—Fiction.
5. German Americans—Fiction. 6. New York (N.Y.)—History—1898–1951—Fiction.] I. Title.
PZ7.W46856Un 2006
[Fic]—dc22   2005015853

Published in the United States by Dutton Children's Books,
a division of Penguin Young Readers Group
345 Hudson Street, New York, New York 10014
www.penguin.com/youngreaders
Designed by Irene Vandervoort
Printed in USA   First Edition
10 9 8 7 6 5 4 3 2 1

In memory of Ms. Renée Perrin,

taken too young, and for all

who perished on the *General Slocum*—

May They Rest in Peace

Where there's money going, there's always someone to pick it up.

———

Episode 10—Wandering Rocks

Ulysses by James Joyce

Reference to the *General Slocum* tragedy

Acknowledgments

I would like to thank Maureen Sullivan and Richard Abate for their faith in me; Vanessa and Carl, Alexander and Benjamin, for their stalwart support; and my daughter, Olivia, without whose patience and love I'd still find myself out at sea.

T. K. WELSH

APRIL 11, 2005

HOPEWELL

the UnResolved

PART I

CHAPTER 1

June 15, 1904
The East River, New York City

It was on June 15, 1904, a warm and sunny summer's day, as the clock in City Hall struck nine, that the *General Slocum* cast off from her pier in lower Manhattan, with the blowing of a horn. I remember the busy decks, packed cheek by jowl with women and children, as we strained against the rail to get a better look, dressed in our Sunday best. Nearly all of Kleindeutschland was there; at least that's how it seemed to me. Tomorrow, they'll call it the Lower East Side. At this time, it was Little Germany. We were off to Locust Grove, Long Island Sound, on an outing for St. Mark's Lutheran Church. There would be games and swimming and food; lots and lots of food. And boys. Sunday school was finally over. And ten feet distant, trapped in the crowd like a flea between hairs, stood Dustin, the most beautiful boy in the world. My name is

Mallory Meer. I'd turned fifteen the week before, and in an hour—thanks to the only boy I've ever loved—I would be dead.

I float around the white memorial in Middle Village, Queens, among the other insubstantial figures. We are the unidentified remembered—the unknown, unforgotten victims of the *General Slocum* who continue, unresolved, like Tantalus, to grasp at something slightly out of reach. Over thirteen hundred started that fateful journey on that balmy summer's day. Fewer than three hundred survived. I see the spirits coalesce around the monument like fog. I know their longing and their pain. I'm one of them.

The steamship chugged up the East River, skirting the busy streets and thoroughfares, the piers and docks of New York City. I remember we could actually feel the vessel tilt beneath our feet as we rushed from port to starboard for a look across the river. There was a great shout as the ship's horn faded and a band began to play—romantic German love songs that made my mother slide back into memory as she stared across the starboard beam, between the glistening waves, mesmerized by the river.

She was dressed in a charcoal-colored cotton skirt, ankle-length, with an off-white blouse and wide-brimmed hat, made of straw, with hand-sewn flowers budding from the narrow red-and-yellow band. Her cheeks were crimson from the pressing crowd, the unusually warm weather, the startling humidity. Her blue eyes seemed to take in everything: first, this couple; that man; a woman with a lime green blouse; and then, something unknown and indiscernible at her feet. In her right arm, she clutched my baby sister,

Nixie. At two, Nixie still wore a cotton bonnet that covered most of her face, including her moody brown eyes and golden hair, each strand thin as a spider's thread. She was dressed in the snow-white silk and lace of the family christening gown. It had been passed down by Grossvater Liebowitz, and each of us had worn it, one by one, in turn, at every special and grave occasion, as long as it still fit.

My younger brother, Helmuth, fidgeted nearby. He wore his summer Sunday shorts and a cinder black wool jacket, an off-white cotton shirt—tight in the collar and cuffs—and a gray cap with a brim.

My sister, the shy but beautiful Louisa, only one year and a half more junior than myself, still wore her confirmation dress. She shrank against the mob, fixed to my mother's shadow.

And I . . . I wore my brand-new sea blue skirt, my sister's lavender silk blouse, and my most colorful Easter bonnet. It was the outfit my mother's friends had tsk-tsked at only the week before, noisy as storks. My skirt was so full-bodied that I appeared to carry a train behind me, reminiscent of another age. My stockings were dark and thick. My shoes were corded with so many bindings that only the hundred-handed Briareus could have readily untied them. And it wasn't my sister's lavender silk blouse. Buttoned tightly at the neck and wrist, the smooth material revealed no wayward patch of skin. No. It was the way I looked within it that concerned them: the curve of my budding bustline underneath the soft material; more of a promise than a proof of femininity.

I knew Dustin was coming. I can say it now, and it appeases, soothes the salt that lingers still within my joints and ligaments. We had planned it earlier that week. And he had never seen me in that blouse and sea blue skirt. Such were my thoughts then, the largest of my concerns, as we steamed north through butterscotch sunlight.

The farther we sailed, the less crowded the deck. There were three decks in all—the hurricane, the promenade, and main—open to passengers and the summer elements. At first, nearly everyone had tried to climb the staircase to the topmost hurricane—the deck on which we stood. All hungered for that grand view of Manhattan . . . and the breeze. But now that the *General Slocum* was finally under way, they had begun to disappear below, fanning out in all directions. The band struck up another song. I whispered to my mother that I was feeling faint. "Some water," I muttered vaguely, moving off.

She nodded, tugging at Helmuth. "Please don't be long," she said in German with a note of desperation in her voice. Louisa slipped beside her. She touched my mother gently on the upper arm, confirming her presence.

I moved off toward the funnels and the pilothouse, making my way first down one staircase, then the next, aware the whole time of his presence in my wake, the way he glided down the steps, the movement of his muscles in his clothes on that hot summer day. By the time I had reached the main deck and ducked into another stairwell, Dustin was right behind me.

Time does not matter after death. It seems like all this happened only yesterday, and to me, trapped in this atemporal space, it did. I remember turning at the stairwell that led down to the Lamp Room. I could see Manhattan gliding by, over the brightly painted lifeboats—they looked brand-new—beyond the bulwark and the rail. I descended into darkness, waiting for him, for his promise and my wish to be fulfilled.

Dustin towered over me, though he was but sixteen. He took his cap off with a sweep of his right hand. He smiled almost apologetically and leaned down through the shadows, and as I felt his lips brush up against mine, everything stopped: the steamship; the waters of the river; the blood inside my veins and arteries. I could hear his heart pound next to me. I could feel his lips press down, so soft—smooth as the throat notch of a cat—and everything began again, recharged. I smelled his breath as he pulled back. My foot had turned. My heel had risen slightly outward. I felt a sharp stab in my stomach, as if I'd swallowed a stone. *This is what it's like*, I thought. My first real kiss was less and so much more than anything I'd ever imagined.

That's when Bingham Goldstein first appeared, outside the Lamp Room, flanked by two friends. I pushed Dustin away as they drew near. They could see us clutching in the shadows. Bingham's face grew dark. He stopped and stared, as if to be quite certain. He wore a smooth black bowler, pulled down in front, tilted sharply to one side. It seemed to cast an impossibly long shadow for such a small hat. His lips retreated from his teeth. His gums were glimmering. "This is a juicy pie," he said, rubbing his hands together. "Mallory Meer and Dustin Bauer. Caught in a kiss." Then his face grew grim.

"That's Brauer," Dustin said.

Bingham turned toward his two friends—fat Abelard Warner and skinny Karl Lehman—and laughed. *Brauer* means brewer in German; *Bauer* means peasant. It was Bingham's little inside joke. He'd been telling it for years. He reached into his hand-stitched, dark brown suit and took out his cigarettes. "Had I known what kind of girl you are," he said, looking pointedly at me, "I would have made an effort."

"Be careful, Goldstein," Dustin said.

"You tried hard enough . . . hard enough for me to say no," I tossed back at him. Dustin was standing up for me, for me! And against Bingham! Dustin's father, Arvin, worked for Bingham's father—the venerable Otto Goldstein, who owned the Golden Rose, the finest beer garden in Kleindeutschland.

Bingham lit his cigarette. The match glowed briefly and was gone. "Tainted meat now," he said. Then he turned and added, "We should leave them to their lovemaking. Kleindeutschland needs new workers, as my father always says. But be warned, Mallory: We're on a St. Mark's outing. And this one, if he hasn't told you, is a Jew."

Dustin moved forward, muttering an oath, his hands balled up into fists, but I caught him by the jacket. It was difficult to hold him back. The old and frayed material began to tear. He was so strong that I almost couldn't hold him. Bingham and his two friends—like mismatched bookends—scurried down the hall, and after a moment, Dustin relaxed. He settled his back against me, and as he turned, to my surprise, I could see his eyes were watering. I didn't know what to say. The moment of that kiss had passed. It was behind me now, another monument along the path. And my mother would be worried about me. I patted Dustin awkwardly on the shoulder and hurried out the door.

Dustin stood there for a moment longer without moving, tucked in the shadows, following me with his eyes. When I was no longer visible, he pulled out his tobacco pouch and carefully rolled a cigarette. He cocked it in a corner of his mouth. He struck a match. For a moment, in the halo of the light, his features were illuminated. The delicate eyebrows—those of a scholar, as I'd described them to my sister, two months earlier. The Gypsy black eyes. The strong nose and full mouth with the slightly feminine red lips. And then that jaw, where I imagined—later—he stored up all his anger and his pride. So firm and confrontational. So ultimately decisive. A tear appeared on Dustin's cheek, the match fell from his hand, and he was gone.

It was a while before we saw the smoke. We were sailing past Wards Island, beyond Hell Gate, when it began to billow from a forward hold. But it was only later that I witnessed how it happened. By then, I was already dead. And underwater. And, for the most part, upside down. But I could still see where the hull appeared most blackened by the now-extinguished flames.

Through the waving arms and legs, like giant sea anemones, bloated, albino-skinned or black as tar, shiny and naked . . . although, if you looked carefully, you could still see tiny hairs on the dead skin, rippling like rabbit fur in a breeze. Through the open mouths, the incinerated arms and legs, I saw precisely how that careless spark first set ablaze that single box of straw. It was alight in seconds. No, it wasn't the ship's stove cooking chowder, as many speculated at the inquest. The flames, fueled by the air blown down the stairwells, began to stretch and spread around the storage space. The Lamp Room, as the crew referred to it, ballooned with fire. The door began to bow. Wood squealed as water steamed. Smoke puffed and whinnied through the crack between the door-jamb and the door, slithering topside through the stairwells, gasping for air.

A pair of seamen in the galley smelled the smoke before they saw it. They looked at each other and started down the hallway at a run. Without even thinking—and devoid of training, as it turned out—they opened the door to the Lamp Room. This was exactly what the fire craved. Nursed by a fresh inhale of oxygen, the fire scrambled up the stairs. The crewmen tried to put it out. They flailed at the flames with their clothes, but it was useless. The open passage of the stairwell served as a chimney. The fire shot across the main deck, paused for a moment, and then ran along the bulkheads to the ceiling. Passengers burned. They bolted in all directions, screaming, tearing at their clothes, some leaping overboard. Others tugged at lifeboats. But the *Slocum* was traveling too fast to lower them; not safely, anyway. And besides, they were lashed to the deck, pinned down with metal clips. They wouldn't budge.

Ten minutes passed before the crew dared tell the captain. He was in his fo'c'sle, enjoying a cold glass of pale ale, compliments of the Golden Rose. It took him another three minutes to make it to the pilothouse. Then, instead of steaming shoreward—to Manhattan, Queens, to Wards or Randall's Island—he headed north. "The shoreline was busy with oil tanks," he affirmed later at the inquest, to everyone's astonishment. "I feared a secondary blaze." A secondary blaze! We steamed northward, toward North Brother Island, funneling the wind down the stairwells, fueling the flames. The fire spread first to the promenade, and then to the hurricane deck. The stairwells were littered with bodies, choked with fire and smoke. Passengers streamed toward the stern, snatching life vests from the ceiling as they moved. But the shoulder straps were mostly rotten. As mothers fought over them, like rabid dogs, the life vests crumbled in their hands. Some lashed them to their children anyway and tossed them overboard with anxious prayers. Others cowered as the flames drew near. Deckhands turned on gray fire hoses, but they burst like overstuffed sausages. The crowd yanked them from their hands. Nothing worked. Anyway, it was too late.

Those who had not been burned alive, or overcome by smoke, had leaped across the rails already, into the choppy waters of the river. Most simply could not swim and drowned after only a few seconds. A precious few grabbed floating debris—one boy a wooden hobbyhorse—and tried to stay afloat until the fleet of vessels gathering in our wake could pick them up.

I remember standing on the hurricane deck, engulfed now in bright orange flames. I remember feeling the heat lick at my skin. I could not find my mother, or my sisters, or my brother. I saw a woman watch her daughter burst into a fire fountain. She wept. We all wept, but our tears evaporated on our cheeks. The river called me, although I could not swim. I'd never learned. It had seemed, well, pointless at the time. I could hear the screams of children blistering. I could smell the stench of burning flesh. I saw a boy climb up onto the after-rail, his golden hair on fire. But he did not leap into the waves. He simply stood there, like a torch. Then he tipped over, broke in half. I saw women not much older than myself burn, blacken, and crumble, their babies pressed against their chests.

I felt the hands of someone pull me from behind. It was Dustin. He was alive! I could see him now, despite the smoke and flames. He was wrestling with a life vest. But it was just too late. Too late, in fact, for nearly all of us. The burning decks gave way, collapsed, and those who remained aboard cascaded down into the opening, through the flooring to the very bottom of the ship, the bilge, an inferno of wood, and rope, and oily rags and canvas, and cords of human flesh. Dustin tumbled off the deck. He was gone, sucked down into the darkness by the frothing waves, only to reappear quite suddenly, scooped up by the steamship's massive paddle wheel, swung round and dropped onto a nearby tugboat. Like providence divine. I was already in the water. I felt the surface tension slip across my face as though it were an undergarment, dressing me for death. My skirt began to suck me down. The water was my outer skin. I could feel it crushing me as the ship slipped underneath the waves. I was trapped. I could not move. Dustin was gone. I was alone, save for the other figures waving in the currents, grist for the running tide. I let the water in, then. Into my mouth and nose. Into my lungs. I let it take me, like a lover, like Dustin wanted to, and should have done. Before. I let the river fill me up.

The steamship bumped, and spun about, and slowly drifted from North Brother to Hunts Point. She groaned and slithered with the current, plowing the seafloor with her keel. Time stopped again. I saw the tiny hairs on distant arms go stiff. Some were still clasping babies. Bubbles refused to rise. Corpses stopped bobbing on the surface. I saw the flames grow still. And then I felt myself begin to tear, out of my very skin, like a butterfly, abandoning my cocoon self, this mortal coil. I felt myself ascend, to fly, to burst across the river, no longer needing to breathe, no longer feeling the weight of my own body. Now, to my vigil.

All this comes back to me, and I remember, like the pattering of raindrops on a window, yet another afternoon—three weeks earlier, it must have been—when Louisa and I had gone to Coney Island. We had wandered through the Hall of Mirrors, seen all the countless versions of ourselves, the possible conclusions.

I do not understand it all. Not yet, at least. I know I have to do something, but what? I have no idea. I can't just stay here, in Middle Village, Queens, trapped between this world and the next.

Nor can I move on to the great beyond until my family and friends have mourned me, until some justice to the guilty has been meted out. It seems that only then will I let go. After the trial and punishment. Only then will a single lifeline settle within time, like the gradually declining hum of a violin string, plucked once, and then released.

Can anybody hear me? Is anybody there?

CHAPTER 2

June 15, 1904
Kleindeutschland, New York City

The news blew like an ill wind through Kleindeutschland, moved like a plague. With a population of only eighty thousand, all knew someone who had been aboard the *Slocum*, or knew someone who knew someone. None could escape. No amount of lamb's blood on the lintel could send the Angel of Death on his way.

The fear was something you could taste. It was palpable. It fell upon you without looking: sitting at your desk; ambling down the street; in school; at home—no matter where you were. It latched on to your bones like the jaws of a ravenous beast. Borne on a wave of tidings, it reached Arvin Brauer as he was brewing yet another batch of the Golden Rose's most infamous pale ale. Hans Miller was the one who broke the news.

Twelve and precocious beyond his years, Hans somehow knew

all things that had an impact on Kleindeutschland—like a contemporary Hermes, messenger of the gods. He appeared, disheveled, as was his wont, wearing a soot black cap, pitched down in front, with a perennial scowl below his periwinkle eyes—bright as the headlights of a distant carriage, looming over a hill. "Meister Brauer," he said. "Meister Brauer," he kept on saying until Arvin shook him by the shoulders.

"What is it, Hans? What's wrong?"

"The *Slocum*," he intoned, as if waking from a dream.

"What about her?" Arvin Brauer's blood grew cold. "What about the *Slocum*?" he repeated.

"She is sunk."

Arvin Brauer leaned on the boy, as much to prop himself up as to pacify young Miller. "How many?"

"How many, sir?"

"How many . . . perished?" Arvin could barely squeeze the words out. His lungs felt as though they had collapsed.

"I don't know," the boy said, adding, "She floundered as she burned. Some jumped, they say. But most were drowned. Some say a thousand, sir. Or more."

"A thousand!" The master brewer took a small step backward. "So many?"

"It may be more by nightfall." Miller had a disconcerting way of fidgeting as he stood, as if he were going to suddenly run off, without warning, on some new errand of extreme importance.

"Dustin," said Arvin. He shook the boy again. "What have you heard about my son? He was on board."

"Nothing," said Miller, backing up. "I'm sorry, sir. But I have others to inform." He held out a tiny hand. "I have to go."

Arvin Brauer slipped a nickel into the messenger's cold fingers. "Thank you," he said, and wondered at the words. He took his apron off mechanically. He donned his coat and black felt hat. He started for the door. It was only when he had ventured out into the street that he remembered that he had failed to quench the boiling vat. This batch of ale would die only half-formed.

I can see the marsh birds flying overhead, the vast wetlands of Schlüsselburg, due south of the mighty Weser River. I can see a far, far younger Arvin Brauer—with the same dark eyes of my love, Dustin—as he moves from one town to the next, tramping from brewing job to brewing job around Westphalia in Lower Saxony. How afraid and yet how strong he was, so much like his own son would become. A Jew amid so many gentiles. And not just any Jew: a Maskilim; a follower of the *Haskalah,* the so-called Jewish Enlightenment, that sprang up like a fountain in the 1770s and coursed across the Jewish mindscape until the later nineteenth century. Inspired by the European Enlightenment that would eventually give birth to the American idea, the *Haskalah* was based upon the "rational." It encouraged Jews to study more than just the Talmud; to learn their local European languages and not just Hebrew;

to enter fields such as agriculture, and crafts, the arts and sciences—even such worldly tasks as brewing beer. The Maskilim attempted to assimilate into European society through dress, through language, manners, and their loyalty to native ruling powers. But it did Arvin Brauer little good. For bundled with his thirst for rationality, with his desire to assimilate and to belong came his enlightened burgeoning belief in the rights of all men to be free, to be treated equally under the law, and to shun the lash of tyranny that creased the land of Prussia.

It was 1888 when Dustin Brauer was born . . . and his mother, Tabea, died. His grandfather—Arvin's father—had recently passed away and, due to the laws of primogeniture and entail, only the eldest of the Brauer clan—firstborn son, Samuel—could inherit the marshy farmland Arvin's father had scraped together from a lifetime of labor in the breweries of Prussia. Even if he had wanted to, Samuel couldn't have shared his small inheritance; the law of entail made it verboten for him to divide up his newly acquired property. Thus, Arvin and the rest of the Brauer boys were left with nothing but their clothes and their father's indomitable will to work.

Following his father's death, Arvin had traveled from his home in Schlüsselburg first east-south-east to Hannover, and then onward to Berlin. It was in the shadow of war and revolution, of Prussian expansionism, of enlightened *Haskalah* and itinerant artisanship, with his sickly wife, Tabea, in tow—now pregnant with

Dustin—that he found himself one day in the company of another young brewer named Jacob Stieglitz, and his life forever changed.

I can see him still, sitting in that worker's hall in West Berlin, enjoying a bowl of chicken soup, when he entered into conversation with the pale-faced Jacob who had just come in from Leipzig to the south.

"I am only here for a little time—perhaps a month," said Jacob, sucking on a bone. "I've already lost two brothers and a sister to the pogroms. And there are precious few master brewers who will hire a Jew, as you'll find out . . . soon enough."

"Where are you going?" Arvin asked.

"To America."

"America!" Arvin had heard of America, of course. But this land of promise and opportunity seemed as elusive and unattainable as Zion—the aspired homeland of all Jews. "But it is so far," he said.

"My granduncle, David, emigrated there some twenty years ago. To Minnesota."

"What is Minn-e-so-ta?"

Jacob Stieglitz laughed. "You are a *Hinterwäldler*, aren't you?"

Arvin was hurt. As a Maskilim, he felt he was better educated than most artisans. "I have studied," he answered rather churlishly. He was no hick.

Stieglitz relented. He dropped his chicken bone into his bowl, glanced about the table, and reached into his ragged coat. "Here," he said, removing a tattered piece of paper. He laid it carefully on the table. The paper was yellowed with age.

It appeared to be some kind of poster with the picture of a great steam locomotive in the center. The word "Wanted" was emblazoned across the top.

"You do know how to read?" Stieglitz said.

"Of course." Arvin picked up the paper. It was a work notice of some kind, issued by . . . it was hard to read the word: the Minn-e-so-ta Territory. **Wanted. Looking for able-bodied men who dream of freedom and a better life to work upon the Northern Pacific Railway.** . . . At the bottom was the flamboyant signature of a man named Eugene Burnand, Commissioner of Emigration.

Stieglitz reached out, picked up the poster delicately, and began to fold it once again. "I know what you're thinking. I know it's old; it was my granduncle's. But it takes a long time to build a railroad across a country like America. I've heard they still need men. What can you do besides brewing?"

Arvin shrugged. "I'm good with my hands. As long as it's honest, I don't care what kind of work I do. My wife is pregnant and . . ."

"Your wife!" said Stieglitz. He rolled his eyes and laughed. "Oh, no. No wives, my friend. They want only men—single men." With that he popped the poster back into his coat. "Come," he added. "They will be calling out the jobs soon." He stood and belched and patted his stomach with a loving tenderness. "If you don't get a spot in front, you don't work," he added blithely. Then he was gone.

Arvin tried to follow him through the busy hall, but Stieglitz disappeared into the throng. He moved like a freshwater eel, gliding between the dirty, coat-clad workers.

Later that night, after failing to secure a new job, after watching dozens of other men all around him picked by the steward, Arvin trudged back to the tiny boardinghouse where he had left Tabea. It was a cold and windy night. The stars swirled in the heavens above him, and he dreamed about the Minnesota Territory. Perhaps, he thought, it would be prudent to travel on alone. Some men left their families behind while they carved out a place for them in the new world. But the idea of leaving the sickly Tabea behind in Germany filled him with dread. Her pregnancy had only made her weaker, and he already felt guilty for making her with child.

He heard the screaming as he turned the corner. The boardinghouse was still a good fifty yards away, but there was no mistaking the sound of Tabea's voice. Arvin sprinted down the cobblestones, punched through the door, and barreled up the stairs. Tabea was lying on the bed in the room they shared with seven other migrant workers. A single candle burned behind her, barely illuminating her heart-shaped face, those dark brown eyes—that would be Dustin's—and her long black curly tresses.

A portly midwife stood beside the bed, her hands blotched red with blood. As he entered the room, the midwife turned. She recognized him instantly. "I did everything I could," she said preemptively. "But the baby . . . he breeched."

Arvin dropped onto his knees. He took his wife's face into his hands and turned her gently toward him. Tabea's eyes were glassy, distant. She seemed to be looking through him at the wall. "Tabea," he whispered, brushing at her hair. "Tabea?"

"She cannot hear you," the midwife said. She wiped her hands across her apron. "You are too late. But here," she said, bending down toward a bundle on the floor. "Your son." She lifted the pile of rags, and Arvin saw him for the first time. Even then, Dustin looked like his mother. He mewed and stirred.

Arvin stared down at Tabea. He felt his heart tear down the center. He closed her eyes. Then, with a mighty sigh, he reached out for the boy. His hands were as heavy as two stones. He drew the baby toward his chest. Dustin stirred and looked up at his father. And even though he knew it was impossible, Arvin felt as though the barely opened eyes rebuked him, saying, "Be careful of what you wish for, Father . . ."

Arvin looked once more at his dead wife, her face pale as white marble. He looked down at his child.

"What will you name him?" said the midwife, trying to change the subject. She began to gather up her things matter-of-factly. Death was a companion to her work. The angel hovered over everyone.

Arvin glanced out the window. It had started to snow. He could see large white flakes descending through the night. "Dustin," he said. "It means dark stone."

All of these events, once simply the fare of table chatter, became known to me as I watched Arvin Brauer stumble through the streets of New York City—first to St. Mark's, then to the city morgue, and finally to the adjacent Charities Pier on Twenty-sixth Street. How they became known to me—as I dangled upside down, pinned to the *General Slocum*—was then and is still a great mystery to me. I simply knew them. I didn't know the Brauer family well, except for Dustin. But as I swept down through the airless streets and found myself inside of Arvin Brauer, all that had made him who he was welled up inside me as my own.

I can still taste the zebra mussels that he had pined for as a young boy every Tuesday evening back in Schlüsselburg, with the flavor of wild onions, and the briny broth Arvin reduced over his potbellied stove in their small house by the Weser River, only a stone's-throw distance from the castle of the Weser Hills, founded by the Minden bishop Gottfried von Waldeck in the fourteenth century. How do I know all this? It is so much, and yet it does not overwhelm me. And the castle, with its bulbous towers and red-tiled roof, how do I know that it was once the residence of the bishops of Minden, named after holy Petrus, the patron saint of the diocese Minden, transformed into a princedom in 1648?

Perhaps I linger in these memories just to avoid the stench of rotting flesh. Perhaps it is to turn away, to block the crowd of relatives, grief-stricken, anxious, or bereft, who gather by the doorway to the warehouse, waiting for their turn to peer at death.

CHAPTER 3

June 15, 1904
Twenty-sixth Street, New York City

The warehouse floor was wet, glazed with the constant dripping of block ice, hauled in to keep decay at bay. It ran the length of two long city blocks. The walls were lined with windows in two rows, triptychs of glass, illuminated trinities, repeating almost endlessly, revealing knots of people gathering, barely formed crowds—a brother here, a father, son, a sister with her children there—the shattered faces peering at the rows of corpses laid out in pine coffins. How strange it was to see the dead already fitted in their Sunday best, as if, instead of readying for a picnic, we had known—somehow—that it would end like this. We were *ausarbeiten*, prepared, decked out and primped and coiffed for death by our own hands.

As Arvin entered the warehouse, an official from the coroner's office stepped up and asked him if he had filled out a death certificate. "What's that?" he said, cracking his reverie. "No," he protested, pushing back. "I mean, I don't know," he continued, moving off. That's when he first saw Otto Goldstein, the owner of the Golden Rose, and next to him, his bowler off, and his eyes puffed up and red from crying, my father—Leonard Meer. Beside them, sitting down, was mother and Louisa, and little Helmuth, safe and sound.

And Nixie. Where was Nixie? But I already knew. All that remained of my baby sister was that scrap of christening gown my mother kept on touching with her fingers, rubbing it over and over and over again, as if—somehow—some genie might appear to grant her wishes at the touch. Beside them lay the smallest coffin I had ever seen, no more than twenty inches long. Like a doll's box, or a toy. Not a real coffin. Something quite make-believe.

"Brauer! Arvin Brauer," Goldstein exclaimed. "What are you doing here?"

Arvin stepped up and took his black felt hat off and bowed a little bow. "My son was on the *Slocum*. Dustin. Didn't you know?"

"You should be at the Rose. Who's tending the vats?" he asked, somewhat perplexed.

"Otto," my father interrupted. "What are you saying?"

A portly man with a bald pate and beady light blue eyes, Goldstein began to sputter something, stopped, and turned away. He was wearing a midnight blue serge suit with a broad straw boater wrapped in red ribbon. His waistcoat was lined with silk thread, silver and crimson and the deepest ocean blue. His Egyptian-cotton shirt seemed to glimmer like gold. His elegant crimson bow tie, wrapped perfectly about his bulbous neck, bobbed up and down each time he swallowed.

In contrast, my father was dressed in the simplest of suits: dark gray with a plain off-white shirt and his favorite blue tie with white stars. As tall and stately as Goldstein was short and stout, my father towered over the scene. His spectacles glimmered with sunlight, like a pair of moons in an alien sky. He laid a hand on Arvin Brauer's shoulder, brought him close. "Ula is lost. I'm sorry, Arvin. I know how you felt about her . . ."

Arvin's heart swelled up with sadness. Ula had been a bright and generous woman, the "bloom of the Golden Rose," as the men who worked at the tavern called her. More than a moderating influence on Otto, she had always served as his moral beacon, a counterbalance to his indifferences. It had been Ula who had persuaded Otto to take a chance on Arvin. She had seen within the bereft Jew from Schlüsselburg a passion for his art matched only by that strange, delightful thing that she had once seen manifested in her father, Conrad Heinemann, the founder and former owner of the Golden Rose, who had built the finest beer garden in Kleindeutschland, only to lose it to Otto Goldstein when he failed to pay his note on time. Ula had worked hard then to seduce her father's banker. She had burned dozens and dozens of meals to master his favorite dishes, for it was well known even then that Otto Goldstein was a man who liked to eat. She had swooned effortlessly at his lifeless recitations of Goethe. She had flirted and reclined, flanked and parried into confrontation. And best of all, she made Otto think that each of her seductions was *his* move, of *his* design and authorship, of *his* most masterful dominion. Less than twelve months after her father had lost the deed to the Golden Rose, Ula found it tucked up inside her trousseau, pinned by red needles and bound in waxy ribbon, the only wedding present she had asked of her new husband. Old man Heinemann died four months hence.

Arvin looked over at Goldstein. He had wandered off a bit, and stood, and stared—red-eyed and sightless—down at a pale pine coffin. There she lay; Arvin could see her clearly now. But surely this pasty figure, with the broken lips and purple cheekbone, with the open lifeless eyes of some great cod, this water bag of memory, wasn't Ula.

Just then, Bingham Goldstein slithered into view. He approached his father hesitantly, like a dog whipped one too many times. He looked down at the woman in the coffin and hesitated, brought his fingers to his lips, biting his clenched fist. Otto turned and saw his son for the first time. His body visibly shook, as if he had been struck by some great weight. Goldstein reeled, steadied himself, and drew back portly arms. "Bingham," he sighed. "When I saw your mother, I assumed . . ."

"I'm sorry. I'm so sorry, Father."

"For what?" said Goldstein quizzically. "You are alive. Thank God!" He pressed Bingham's face in his hands. He kissed him gently on the brow.

"Bingham," Arvin Brauer said. "Have you seen Dustin? Is my son . . . ?"

Bingham spun about. "He's alive," he said, but the words came ominously. He stared at his mother in her box. "He may wish otherwise," he added at an angle.

"What does that mean?" my father intervened.

Arvin sighed. "Where is he?"

"It was him," said Bingham, glancing at his father. "His fault. His . . . cigarette."

Goldstein's eyes fell into focus. He stared first at his son and then at Arvin Brauer. "What do you mean, his fault?"

"My fault?" a voice said, and I felt Dustin pass right through me. I felt his legs, his arms, his chest and face. He paused for a moment at the center of my being and then just slid away. He was gone. "What are you saying, Bingham?" Dustin stood by his father, holding him back with one arm. Arvin sighed.

"You know exactly what I'm saying." Bingham glanced up at his father's face. It seemed as though he could not suffer Dustin's stare. "The fire," he continued. "It was *his* cigarette. Father, I saw it." He stared down at his mother's face. "I'm sure he didn't mean it. How could he have known? But he threw it to the deck and walked away. And it kept burning. The deck began to pitch and roll. It rolled and struck that box of straw and . . ."

And then I saw it, too. In my mind's eye. I don't know how I did. But I saw it roll and spark, and sputter as the straw caught, and the fire billowed into life. I watched it delicately attend the Lamp Room walls. That's how it happened. Bingham was telling the truth.

"You're lying." Dustin pulled himself up to his full height. He took a step closer to Bingham. "You're lying; tell them."

"I'm sure he didn't mean to do it," Bingham said. "It was an accident."

"I'm sure," said Goldstein. He turned and looked on Dustin with such venom that the boy stepped back unconsciously. "But for Ula and for everyone else. There must be a reason. Someone must be responsible. Fires don't start themselves."

"Who is responsible?" a man with a chocolate-colored bowler added, stepping in. His eyes took in first one face, then another. "Who did you say started the fire? What's his name?"

"Dustin Brauer," Goldstein said.

"Now wait a minute," Arvin said. He took a step closer to Goldstein, his palms stretched out before him. "We don't know what happened. Who can be sure? You're just upset, Herr Goldstein."

"Are you saying my son is a liar?" Goldstein moved a step closer. "Why, you ungrateful Jew . . ."

"Jew?" the man in the chocolate-colored bowler said. "He's a Jew?"

"Let's all just take a breath," my father said. "We're all upset; that's understandable. I've lost my Nixie and my Mallory. Otto, you've lost your Ula. We've all lost someone. It's natural to look for something, someone to blame. But we need to think, to reflect and—"

"He's a Jew," Goldstein said. "And his son, too. Dustin Brauer."

The man in the bowler turned toward the woman behind him. She was trying to overhear the conversation. Everyone began to turn in their direction. "A Jew started the fire," someone said. "Did you hear?" someone echoed in turn. "His name's Dustin. Dustin Brauer."

"He shouldn't have been on the *Slocum*," someone said. "On a Lutheran outing, what's a Jew doing there? Did you hear?" she continued.

"A Jew, Dustin Brauer. Burned the *Slocum*."

"Who killed my wife?" someone cried.

"Who killed my daughter?"

The questions ascended like the crowing of cocks, from one mouth to the next, air light, lifting the blanket of grief that smothered the room. *It was him*, someone said. *A Jew. A Jew set the* Slocum *on fire. Dustin Brauer. Dustin Brauer.* The words billowed like flames, licked the air. *Dustin Brauer killed my wife. Dustin Brauer burned my baby. Dustin Brauer. Dustin Brauer. Jew.*

Arvin corralled his son up in his arms. He began to move away, back toward the entrance to the pier. Then, without warning, he just ran, pulling Dustin in his wake. They jostled together through the gathering crowd and disappeared out the door.

For a moment, no one spoke. Otto Goldstein called his son to his side with a hand signal. My father shifted from one foot to the next, trying to settle his weight. My sister Louisa gathered Helmuth to her thigh and pressed her other hand around my mother's shoulder. And my mother, as she ran her left thumb around that small white piece of fabric, around and around, wearing the christening gown down—all that was left of dear Nixie—as my mother looked up at my father, she said with a smile, "That Dustin. I knew he was no good. I warned you, Leonard. I warned you."

I found myself in the streets after that, unable to bear the sharp words. They crackled like shards in my throat. I couldn't repeat them. I couldn't let them form on my tongue. I flew and I flew into Captain Van Schaick, in the hospital, with his eye bandaged up like a cyclops, moaning at the gods. He knew his career was kaput. He sat on his bed, staring out of the window, filled with a bottomless longing to erase time, to return—once again—as the steamboat first sailed from the pier, to strains from "Birds of Passage" by Foust, a waltz so loaded now, so burdened down by grief that Van Schaick found it virtually impossible to lift his one eye to the sky. He sighed. It was too horrible to contemplate. The stench of burning human flesh, the flames. It was too terrible, indeed.

I flew and I flew and I found myself within the thick walls of the Knickerbocker Steamboat Company, in lower Manhattan, where the piteous Miss Hall sat bereft, tallying columns and columns of numbers. Someone had told her, I could tell. Thoughts of the *Slocum* assailed her. The fire still burned in her head. I could still feel the flames. They crackled with guilt and with pain. Yet she would not look up from her ledger, for fear of what lingered ahead.

I flew and I flew into William O'Gorman, city coroner, as he sat at his late Sunday breakfast, dissecting his plate of mixed grill—two eggs, over easy, and a shot of Scotch whiskey, prix fixe. I felt the strong rush of tobacco as he puffed on his Jamaican cigar.

And he was gone . . . and I was up and falling into someone else, a placid, quiet, empty place: Henry Lundberg of the U.S. Steamboat Inspection Service; still dreaming the same dream he'd dreamed for the last seven weeks since his betrothal to Miss Mabel Smith. In only four days. Four days of liberty—no, irresponsibility. Four days of self-serving bliss before the ax fell and he was no longer free—the tragically beautiful Henry Lundberg.

I could not stand the sweetness of his breath; it smelled of lavender and mint. I could not stand the source of his tumescence, that view of Miss Smith with her leg up, revealing her white upper thigh, and that patch of intolerable longing—that dream of his. I was ready to fly once again when his landlady knocked on the door. "The *Slocum*," she cried. "She is sunk, Master Lundberg. Wake up." Indeed! Wake up, young Henry, and see what you've wrought.

And he rose and he dressed, and made his woolly-headed way with much haste to his offices. I felt him plop down with a thump on his chair. He stared at his desk. And then, with a start, he reached for his phone, saying, "Get me long distance, please, operator. Fire Island 4622. Mr. Frank Allan Barnaby."

And with that, I was gone, through the wire that ran down the street, across lower Manhattan and under the river, the Long Island Sound, to that great house that stood on a hill. The telephone rang and kept ringing. Barnaby stood in a closet, wrapped around his wife's parlor maid, a French girl from Brittany with the hands of a child. He was bonded to her like a vine, until the steady drilling of the phone cut short his deep grunting, and he pulled away and charged down the hall, still half-dressed. *Where were the servants,* he wondered, *when you needed them most?*

Lundberg's voice was remarkably clear. "The *Slocum*'s burned down to the keel," he said with surprising dispassion. "Off the Bronx. We're in trouble."

They talked in soft murmurs thereafter. They whispered until they hung up. Then Barnaby made his way back to the closet where the naked young maid was still waiting. She was shivering alone in the dark. "I must go," he said bluntly. "To the office. Get me my striped charcoal suit."

We returned to Manhattan. We returned to his office, where the piteous Miss Hall still obsessed over columns of numbers. Barnaby looked deep within her eyes with the same electric charge that he had used to seduce Marie-Claire—yes, that was her name—only hours before. Miss Hall barely stirred. "Yes, Mr. Barnaby. As you wish, sir," she said. "Life jackets were already on order."

Where can I go from here? What must I do? And why won't you give me your hand?

CHAPTER 4

June 15, 1904

Twenty-sixth Street, New York City

I went to Dustin, as I always did. I followed him along the streets and avenues; he was unable to mount a streetcar for fear of being recognized and chased along the city thoroughfares back down to Kleindeutschland. When they had finally returned to their tenement, Arvin and Dustin clambered up the stairs with the weariness of mountain climbers, exhausted after a quick ascent.

The main room, the kitchen and bathroom, faced the sitting room, a stilted assemblage of hand-me-down furniture, pilfered from the streets. Dustin collapsed into a chair in the sitting room. He stared out the window at the traffic below.

"It is always the same," Arvin said. "Those who should love you the most desert you the quickest. Even in America." He paced the kitchen floor, burning off steam. "In the old country, at least, you could tell them by their coats. But here . . ." He sneered. "These goyim of New York." Then he stopped and looked down at his son. "Tell me what happened, Dustin."

"It was my fault. I'm sorry, Father," he said. "Perhaps Bingham was right. Mallory, forgive me. Can you ever forgive me?"

It was a cry so plaintive that I felt it fill my breast with undead air. Dustin was crying out for me. For me!

"Don't say that. Don't ever say that again. Do you hear me?" said Arvin. "You are *not* guilty. I know you're not. Never. Promise me. Promise me!"

"All right, I promise." Dustin continued to cry. I felt myself sucked underwater in his tears. I drowned in them. "Mallory," I heard him say once more, before the shaking stopped.

"We should eat something," Arvin said. "Some chicken soup, perhaps. And some bread." He began to root about the larder. "You must be starving."

"Tell me why, Father."

"Tell you what?" Arvin stopped fussing. He stood perfectly still. "Tell you what, Dustin?"

"Everyone I love. Everyone who comes close to me dies," said Dustin. "First mother. Now Mallory. Everyone I love."

"Please, don't, Dustin. You know that isn't true." Arvin sidled over to his son. He ran a hand around his neck. He drew him close. Dustin settled for a moment in the enclave of his father's chest, then shook his shoulders like a dog. "Leave me alone. Do you want to die, too? Is that what you want?" he said.

Arvin circled the table. He hesitated. He stopped. He looked down at his son, then leaned, the slightest distance, forward. He cocked his head, as though listening for a distant sound—the hoot of an owl between branches. "You will not lose me, Dustin," he said matter-of-factly. "No matter what. God will see to that."

Dustin's eyes went wide. He stood up slowly, painfully. Like an old man. He pushed his chair in underneath the table. He started for the door. "God has enough to see," he answered quietly. "He's been busy all day."

He wandered out of the apartment and began to climb the stairs up to the roof. The landlord, old man Wallenberg, had made a great production of his landings and his stairs. Painted pastoral scenes adorned each sconce and window treatment. The tenement was not called the Delancey Gardens for nothing; as if the name would somehow help the residents forget the roaches and the smell, the paper-thin walls, the shrill parade of other people's lives.

The tenement at 97 Delancey Street provided Wallenberg with an ample source of income and would, eventually, enable him to move to Astor Place. It had been the biggest gamble of the tailor-turned-landlord's life, for he had spent roughly $8,000 of his hard-earned cash to complete the building. He imagined the thousands of pricked fingers, the hundreds of blossoms of blood he had endured throughout the years, down on his knees, pinning the cuffs of other men. His nest egg was full of blood. But the gamble had paid off. In 1890, Wallenberg's personal wealth had stood at only $1,800. By 1904, the value of his real-estate holdings alone had ballooned to $25,000. He finally sold the property on Delancey Street in 1906, raking in more than $39,000 for the five-story building.

A 700 percent return, I calculated. Almost. But why, and how? Mine had never been a head for numbers. How strange. How odd! What did I care for real-estate investments, for finance? No. It was Dustin's head. It was he who calculated and configured. It was he whose mind's eye dwelled upon the landlord, Wallenberg, adding up his actions and inactions, tallying patterns and plans. His brain performed each calculation effortlessly, as easily as his legs pumped as he hurried up the stairs, ever higher, as he climbed the last few rungs of the small ladder, and he was out, and free, and on his own.

Dustin wiggled out of the small hatchway. He breathed the twilight air. There, in the distance; he gathered up some wayward molecules of smoke. He spun about and stared out to the east and north. He could still see the black plume of the *Slocum* as she burned, bobbing and bouncing, drifting from North Brother Island to Hunts Point.

The boat herself was out of sight, reclined behind some other tenement. But the smoke rose skyward through the distant clouds. Like a prayer—a kind of reaching out and upward. A kind of plea.

Dustin's shoulders sagged. He sighed. I could feel him think of me, or who he thought I was. I could see the image brighten in his head. I was smiling and running just ahead of him, just out of reach, down a sidewalk along Stanton Street. I was turning, looking back, and my smile was broken by slim wisps of ebony hair, flying backward in the breeze. My eyes looked like they were on fire. My cheeks were flushed. I was out of breath for looking at you, Dustin. I could barely breathe, I was so in love. And you could see it in my eyes. You knew, Dustin. You knew!

What am I to do with this? All that I see, so many birthday presents. I cannot open them all.

By the time Otto and Bingham Goldstein returned to their apartments above the Golden Rose, it was almost midnight, and it was dark. The servants had lit the light in the entrance to the tavern. Peter, the youngest of his housekeeper's four children, slept on the stairs with a blanket on his legs. He was waiting for the master of the house. He was there to offer him a towel and bowl of water.

The Goldsteins came in without speaking. Peter could sense the silence between them like something you could touch. It was membranous and fleshy. It stretched when you pressed it in the center. It was invisible, but it was there. He handed them both a towel, waited as they washed their hands, and then dashed back into the shadows. The Goldsteins removed their coats, and Peter crept back into view only long enough to grab them. It wouldn't pay to tarry on this night; the masters were out of sorts.

Otto Goldstein stepped into his private dining room. There was a small bottle of schnapps on the carving table. He snatched it up and wrestled with the cork. Bingham scurried through the darkness toward the rear stairwell when he heard his father say, "Where are you going? I want to talk with you."

Bingham stopped. He spun about in the darkened corridor and made his way back toward the dining room. His father was standing by the fireplace. A few embers still burned in the hearth, and he warmed his glass in the glow. "Come here, Bingham."

Bingham crept into the room. He moved toward the head of the table and then paused by the chair to the right. This was his seat. He was used to the world from this angle. He sat down and folded his hands.

"Tell me what really happened." Goldstein spoke without turning. He continued to stare at the fire.

And Bingham repeated the tale. How Dustin had made his way into the Lamp Room to get away from the crowd—the Lutherans. How he had tossed his burning cigarette to the deck, how the steamship had rolled, and the cigarette had spun along the planking toward that box of straw. How it had burst apart, the bright head sputtering like a Roman candle, how it had leaped into the straw and eaten it, consumed it piece by piece with bright fire. How it had licked the walls and climbed like some incendiary ivy, up the bulkhead, up, up. Reaching for the sky. And how he had just run, then, simply run. He hadn't even tried to put the fire out.

"And you were there the whole time? You witnessed the entire thing?"

Bingham straightened, played with his shirt. "Yes, Father."

"This is not some trick, Bingham. I will not suffer them again, your tricks. I'm warning you. This is the truth this time?"

"It is. I swear. I'm not lying." And then most cutting of all: "Mother would have believed me."

"Indeed," said Goldstein. He took another swig from his glass. He spun the liquid around. "It's time you were in bed. You've had a hard day, Bingham."

"What about you, Father?"

"I'll be right there."

Bingham turned and vanished out the door. Goldstein could hear his footsteps as he climbed the stairs. They echoed through the tavern.

Goldstein surveyed his establishment through the door. It was a grand spectacle, to be sure. With three private dining rooms, an expansive beer garden, and a forty-foot bar and salon, the Golden Rose was the queen of Kleindeutschland. No other beer garden in the district could compare. Each room was painted with scenes of the old country: great fields of grain with haystacks towering; majestic river valleys, dotted with castles; the Rhine, in all her splendor, studded with boats; black forest, rugged mountaintop, step-cut by ice. The furniture was an exact replica of what Goldstein had once seen at the Brass Bull in Hamburg: sturdy and dependable; decisive and yet, ultimately, unobtrusive. It was all these things that made the Golden Rose the flower of Kleindeutschland. But there was something else. Otto finished his glass of schnapps. He stared down at the fire. And that was the problem. For, in the end, the Golden Rose was her beer. It was why men came from throughout New York to see her. It was why the crowds waited to be served, packed tight like herring in a crate, each Saturday. It was her dream, her promise, and her fulfillment. And none was more famous than the tavern's pale ale, the beer that had made Goldstein a legend. He had gotten rich off of that recipe. And it wasn't even his. It belonged to that Jew, Arvin Brauer. He had arrived one day on the stoop with that batch of fresh yeast and a longing in his heart. And Ula had invited him in. She had seen the promise in that bowl covered with blue cloth. That yeast! That golden yeast! It was the goose that laid the golden egg, that helped ferment uncounted vats of ale, which each day made him richer. Goldstein stood back from the fire. He glanced at the portraits lined up along the mantel. Their features seemed to move and quiver in the lambent firelight. He picked up his portrait of Ula. She was smiling at him demurely. It was a false pose. There had never been anything demure about Ula. She had engaged demurely, from time to time, when it served her purpose, but she was not demure. She was too busy attending to her diffidence and self-effacement to be demure. . . .

It hurts to be so self-deluded. It burns. I can feel it like the sting of countless insects swarming in my heart. I cannot stay here. It hurts to be in Otto Goldstein.

Goldstein arched his back. He felt his body shudder, and he put the portrait back. He straightened the edges to line them up with the lip of the mantelpiece. It did not pay to have things out of place. He looked down at his dead wife, smiled, and said, "I'm sorry, Ula."

My parents' rooms were humble. We lived in a tenement on Chrystie Street. We shared three rooms, all six of us—well, four, now. Although Nixie hadn't taken up much room. And I generally slept in the sitting room, in my father's chair. The bed in the rear sleeping room was so big that it left only the smallest passageway along one wall where you could stand and change your clothes before climbing in. There was only one bed, and we shared it all. We shared it all, and it was wonderful!

The main room was also the kitchen. It smelled of potatoes and cabbage. No matter how fastidiously my mother cleaned, the odor never quite retreated. The landlord had installed plumbing only a few years earlier, and there was running water and a metal sink. We still had to share the bathroom in the hallway with our neighbors, but we didn't mind. Simply having running water was incredible to my father. To him, running water represented the kind of luxury most commonly associated with the ruling classes. Such things were not meant for simple men.

Father, I loved you so much when I was alive. How unsurprising that I would love you even more now, when I am in your skin. You don't have to prove a thing to me. You never did.

He sat there quietly, in the adjoining room—my father. He was reading a book by a man named Gillette called *The Human Drift*. It was a tiny printing; there wasn't much of a call for such utopian thinking. Gillette longed to create a people's paradise. How ironic that when his book failed—and it would—he would invent the safety razor, transforming products for the first time into disposable commodities. He'd invent consumer dependence, and—as a result—create a fortune for himself. Even my father—the stalwart socialist he was—would adopt his safety razor in a year or two, abandoning forever the little tufts of paper he used to patch himself up with after shaving.

My sister and Helmuth lounged together on the floor beside my father's feet. Mother sat on the small settee, beside my father's reading chair, trying to sew. It was like any other night; yet it was different. I wasn't there this time. Neither was Nixie. Nixie was nowhere to be seen. We were two shadows, cast without shape. We were just memories. Like phantom limbs.

My mother rubbed her patch of christening gown. "As I foretold you," she said.

"'We are all spirits and are melted into air,'" my father said. He pursed his lips. "I'm sorry. As you foretold me."

"As I foretold you," she continued, "I saw it even then."

"Please stop it, Minna. You'll drive yourself mad. Think of the children."

"It's the children I was thinking of. Of Mallory, your daughter. He tried to make love to her for months—your young apprentice." She laughed, and he felt a sudden fear as he watched her lip curl over pearly teeth.

"Dustin's a good boy. No matter what young Goldstein says. And a good watchmaker. I know him, Minna. I work with him every day." My father shook his head. "I tell you, Minna: He doesn't know how to be that negligent. It's just not in his nature."

"First he wormed his way into your heart. Then he tried worming his way into your daughter's heart. Who's next? No, I stand by what I said. Bingham was too good for Mallory, but not that dirty little Jew."

"Minna, please!"

"Shut up! Both of you!" Louisa screamed. "Just be quiet!" She pressed her palms to her ears.

"Louisa," my mother said. She was incredulous. She had never heard her daughter speak this way before. Neither had I.

Louisa got up from the floor. "All day long, everyone's been blaming Dustin. I can't stand it anymore. So what if he's a Jew. He's ten times the boy Bingham is." She started to cry. "Mallory is gone. And Nixie, too. Must we lose everyone?"

My father stood and wrapped his arms about her. Louisa collapsed. "I'm sorry," he said. "My little flower." He brushed his fingers through her hair. "It's late. Why don't you put your brother to bed? We'll be right there."

Louisa lifted Helmuth to his feet. My brother was silent and obedient, for once. I think Louisa's outburst must have frightened him. They vanished into the rear room and closed the door.

Now there was no more procrastination. No more distractions or delays.

"That dirty little Jew, as you call him, is my protégé," Father said, looking down. "He was and is my best apprentice, my only apprentice now, Minna. There are things he can do with his hands that I can't even remember I've forgotten. I'm no longer young; look at me. Look at me, Minna! My eyes have aged before the rest of me."

"I warned you, Leonard."

"Yes, my dear," my father said. He bowed his head. "You warned me. Over and over and over. Come now. Let's go to bed. This day has been long enough."

"What about Mallory and Nixie. They can't go to bed."

My father shuffled over to the candle on the mantel and picked it up. "They are already sleeping."

No, I'm right here, I heard myself reply, but it was voicelessly. I watched my parents make their way into the back room. I saw them close the door, only to see Louisa reappear. She crept across the kitchen to the sitting room. She made her way to the window. She opened it, and a summer breeze washed over her. She looked northeast, at the night sky. The smoke was hidden now, black on black. Louisa sighed. I could feel a solitary tear begin to well up in the corner of her eye. I could feel it gather force, descend, and run across her cheekbone. She was crying for me. I could see it as she shuddered in the dark. I could feel the heaving of her chest. She was crying for me! Until, with one great sigh, she hung her head, she closed her eyes and whispered almost out of reach, "Dustin."

PART II

CHAPTER 5

June 16, 1904
Kleindeutschland, New York City

It's odd what you abandon when you die. Things that before seemed vitally important, momentous, fade and wither. And yet small things, too small to keep in memory—the slightest turning of the wrist, a wink, a nod—live on forever. Life is a line of little things.

Now that I'm dead, I look upon the year 1904 with equanimity. Some people linger in the certainty: that warm June afternoon ruined countless lives, and it did. Of course it did! But carried like seeds, like thistles on a stocking, attached to all that pain, dreaming of rain, were countless opportunities that sprang up from the void. They say nature abhors a vacuum. So does good fortune if you let it come.

By the end of the year, Kleindeutschland was no more. We drove them out, Nixie and me, and all the rest of us. How could you stay when every corner of the street reminded you of your dead wife, your daughter, sister, mother, aunt, your former life? Within a year, nearly everyone in Kleindeutschland was gone, moved away, relocated. They ran to Yorkville, or to the countryside, or to some other state. We haunted them away.

Yet so much more transpired. In 1904, a man invented the ice-cream cone at the World's Fair in St. Louis. There were the first engagements of the Russo-Japanese and the Herero wars. So many things began or ended: the opening of the first New York City subway line; the conclusion of construction for the first tunnel underneath the Hudson River; the manufacture of the very first Rolls-Royce. How wonderful! While one man dreamed up ice-cream cones, another invented the caterpillar track, which was to revolutionize all future wars.

I can feel the balance more than I perceive it. Even the fire itself resulted in unknowable and unanticipated good. Because Kleindeutschland was emptied, two people avoided death. One, a Mrs. April Kleiner, would have been run over by a streetcar in two months over on Houston Street. It's true. I can see her head split open on the cobblestones, the life rushing out of her. All of that blood and brains. But she didn't, or she won't die. It's hard to say. How do you anchor life when time itself is cast adrift? And the other, a man named Henry Slope, would have been murdered. Robbed first, and then murdered, right there, before me, in the street. But Henry wasn't there to be robbed and murdered. Because of me, and Nixie, and so many others who died that day,

Henry was in Peekskill on that fateful afternoon. He failed to attend his execution. He was, somehow, reprieved.

And in a darkened auditorium, I can see flickering lights. I hear hushed voices under music. I see the events of that day flashing across a screen: in a movie called *Manhattan Melodrama,* starring Clark Gable, William Powell, Myrna Loy, and Mickey Rooney— who played the Gable character as a child. It was filmed quickly, designed to turn a modest profit at the most . . . certainly not to set the public mind ablaze, which it did. The film's success surprised the studio and gave a big boost to the careers of both Loy and Powell.

How could I be angry with Louisa? When there is so little love in this world, how could I begrudge my sister a small piecrust of happiness? Jealousy makes no sense when you are dead. In fact, now all of those feelings—hatred and jealousy, anger and pride— seem, well, beside the point; not bad or evil, malevolent or vile, not morally bankrupt, but tasteless and rather bland. Unbeautiful, I guess. Yes, that's it. Not ugly; just unbeautiful. Perhaps I'd known about her secret love for Dustin all along. It's hard to say now. Or, perhaps, I'd been too caught up in my own feelings to see or care about her sentiments. That would have been like me. Not that I was selfish, mind you; just self-preoccupied. I wasn't bad or mean, insensitive or vain. No, none of that. I was just . . . alive.

I sit beside my stone memorial in Queens. I sit and wait and watch. I see the things that happened, or were to happen, or might someday transpire . . . You could go mad with your fingers in this knot. There is no certainty in this continuum, and yet all is connected. Each reality, each scene, can be played out, or just as easily revoked. The slightest thing, the smallest wink or nod or turning of the wrist, and ships burn. All perishes to make room for the new.

New York was overcome with grief. I could see that; that was preeminently clear. I could see black bunting raised and wrapped round City Hall by Mayor George McClellan Jr., son of the controversial Union army general. Each flag in New York State was lowered to half-mast. I could see the Reverend Haas of St. Mark's Church weeping over the death of his wife in his back rooms, and yet still finding time for others who had lost so much. I could see stacks of coffins being unloaded outside the various undertakers of Kleindeutschland. Since so many parishioners had died, the Reverend Haas had decided that there were to be no funerals at St. Mark's Church. Instead, all services were to be conducted in funeral parlors or in private homes. And I could see my father mounting two white ribbons on the front door of our tenement on Chrystie Street—*tap, tap*—white for children—*tap, tap*—beside dozens and dozens of black ribbons, flapping like crows' wings in the summer breeze.

It was at this time that I was finally torn loose from the wreckage. The diver's name was Fitzgerald, William A. He had come over a few years earlier from Galway, and worked first as a riveter in Boston before learning how to weld, and then to dive, and then to weld while diving. He's the one who finally tore me lose. He grabbed me by the shoulders and heaved, and I just came undone, tore down the center of me. He brought me topside and laid me out, just another body on that raft, floating with all those other rafts. We simply lay there in the sun, trying to dry off. My body was crushed beyond recognition, my face ravaged by crabs. *Who are you?* I asked, looking down. *What happened to your pale blue eyes?* Once upon a time, there was a boy who thought me beautiful. Dustin, do you remember? I'll let you go if you promise you'll never forget.

CHAPTER 6

June 18, 1904
Middle Village, Queens

They gave it the name Black Saturday. An enormous crowd gathered at the funeral of the Reverend Mrs. Haas; it was almost like the coronation of a queen. Everyone wore something new. No one, it seemed, could stand to look at that old dress again, that old suit hanging in the closet. Not any longer. They were all tainted now, those clothes, with memories.

Hundreds of victims were memorialized that day, drawn in by cart and horse-drawn carriage to the Lutheran Cemetery, Middle Village, Queens, where, even now, the memorial spins, hazy, in the air; cool, white marble; waiting to be built. Dozens of men in dark suits carry tiny homemade coffins underneath their arms. They spill along the streets. So many undertakers charged such extortionate rates that most of the people of Kleindeutschland were forced to plane home-fashioned coffins on their dining tables after work. They were so small, so delicate, those doll boxes. They looked so tiny in their arms.

And then it was my turn. I saw my mangled body being lowered down, the frightful lip of that mass grave—great hole for the unrecognized remembered. I felt my torso slide, my legs unfold beneath me. Legs wrapped about yet other limbs, despite our individual coffins. And arms and fingers, intertwined. That's how I finally stumbled onto Nixie. What was left of her was propped up underneath another girl so that it was hard to tell where one began and the other finished. They had been baked together by the fire. My sister sat there, looking so nonchalant, without fear, without the slightest trepidation. I caught her eye, and I could feel her smile. She recognized me with a nod. I nodded back, but she was off already, already someplace else, snuggling up against somebody else's soul.

Beyond the waving limbs, I looked up, and I could just make out the crowd, lining the lip, gazing down as if at hell itself. They looked afraid. Was that the word? They looked so . . . mortal. So I reached out to them, to give them comfort, but my arms slipped through them like a memory, and I held nothing; just the unknown. What might have been? What might have been? If you say it three times, will it be?

My mother and father, Helmuth and Louisa, stood off to the side, as if staring down into that pit would render their feelings too clear. They stood apart. They stared at everything and anything that wasn't there, directly in front of them—right there. This hole! Could you see me in this hole?

The earth is wet and cool. It isn't what I imagined it would be. Not fearsome, dank. Not darkly claustrophobic. It's like a blanket tucked around your neck. It does not smother or encumber. It does not hold you down. I'm wrapped inside the bosom of the earth. I'm safe. Protected. Below my stone memorial. Far from uncertain, and yet still unresolved. Our heads float through the clouds. Our feet splay clay.

I could see Bingham and his father, Otto Goldstein. It made me shiver to remember. It had not been fun in him.

I saw our neighbors from downstairs, their neighbors and their neighbors' neighbors. Nancy and Gretchen. And Frederick from school, and his mother, too. His father was but three corpses down, observing the ceremony with the detached self-consciousness that's generally reserved exclusively for atheists. He found the whole thing . . . well . . . amusing. And Klaus and Eric and Mathilda, with that birthmark shaped like a sea horse on her left breast. And Mrs. Kemp, the butcher's wife, and her two daughters, the twins. They're all in here, beside me.

I could even feel Dustin. I could feel him peering out at me from behind that poplar. Watching and waiting. Watching and waiting. But for what? For some release? He was thinking of me. He could see me running still on that warm summer's day, my head turned, and that wisp of jet-black hair between my teeth. I will run with you forever, Dustin.

And I could feel my sister looking, too, and spotting you; the way you stood there, slightly bent, peering out from between green branches. A little comical. Perhaps because you were the least clownlike of all of us. You were the most preoccupied, most serious. The most intense.

I remember the day I confronted you at school and called you melancholy. You stood there for such a long time after that, up against that wall, just thinking. You smiled and shrugged and said, "Aware, not melancholy. Sometimes I wish I weren't. I wish I were more like you."

"Like me?" I answered, fishing.

"Hearing instead of listening. Being instead of becoming. Living—not just alive. I don't know. You're . . . you."

I could have eaten you, just then, right there and then. I could have popped you right into my mouth like some boiled sweet, a sugar ball, like caramel on the tongue. You were the first and only boy who ever made me feel so special. I'd heard such things from my father, of course—so many times, in fact, that they no longer sounded real. But when you talked with me that way, I was no longer "one of the Meer girls." Nor just another winsome student from St. Mark's. We stood outside Kleindeutschland. We were New Yorkers, plain and simple, dreaming the dream of America. And I became yours.

Louisa was standing by you now. She had wandered off and stood beside you by the poplar. You were both whispering. You weren't looking at her—not directly, anyway; you were staring at the ceremony. But you were talking to her. You were talking, and she stood quite still, her head cocked, intent on every word, each syllable. I could see your lips move. The words were lost—too many voices murmured—but I could see them forming words: pressed tight, and oval; little "ohs" and "ahs" and "oohs."

"Get out of there," my mother said. "Louisa, get away. At once."

The Reverend Haas looked gravely down his nose. He was not used to being interrupted. He looked back at his Bible. A visible ripple shifted through the crowd. There were hundreds of people at the ceremony. They'd come from all over New York. Dressed in their Sunday best on Saturday, they already felt out of place. They carried the guilt of the survivor on their backs. It lined their overcoats. They shifted their feet and sighed collectively, a great gray mass of grief.

"Get away from him."

Louisa startled like a deer. She stepped back without thinking, almost tripping on the path. Dustin reached out with his right hand to steady her.

"Keep your hands off my daughter. There's blood on those hands. Keep them away, you dirty Jew. Was Christ's blood not enough?"

"Minna!" my father cried.

The Reverend Haas had found his place. "'In the sweat of thy face shalt thou eat bread, till thou return unto the ground; for out of it wast thou taken: for dust thou art, and unto dust shalt thou return.'" He looked desperately about his flock but he'd already lost them. They'd been submerged in a different melodrama. The crowd was watching my mother carrying on.

"He killed your sister Mallory. And Nixie, too. Burned them alive. Murderer." She turned and faced the great gray mass. "Are you just going to stand there?" She pointed at Dustin in the trees. "He's there. Right there. Look! The Jew who murdered your wives. Who killed your daughters and your sisters. Murderer! Is there not one brave man amongst you?"

That's when the earth moved underneath me. I felt the tremor and the tear. Between the shifting and the opening up, the deck simply gave way. We slipped at first, then slid, all of those arms and legs, like clumps of chicken skin and fat choking a drain. Into the earth. Into the wet red earth. *The Jew who murdered your wives . . .*

Louisa began to walk back down the path. She looked transfixed. She glowed. Everyone stared at her. No one knew what to do. They'd never seen her look that way before. "No one murdered Mallory," she said. "Nor Nixie. Unless, perhaps, the steamship company. They died, Mama, that's all. We all need to accept that."

And the earth stopped sliding downward. I felt myself begin to rise, to spin above the ground like some great samara, a whirligig, just hovering, just out of reach, on some late-summer twilight breeze. Looking down from my memorial.

That's all, Mama. That's all that happened. We just died.

William O'Gorman, the coroner, laid his head down on his desk, buried his fleshy face within his giant alabaster arms, and moaned. The knowledge that an inquest was unavoidable languished like gravity on his frame. Despite, or because of, his massive shoulders, his bulbous bi- and triceps, his beefy neck, he felt crushed, completely inundated, as if he were sitting at the bottom of the sea. He could barely breathe. He had not slept in four days, and it was starting to show.

"All right," he finally said to the jackal-like man in the corner.

The man grinned, prestidigitating perfect teeth. He had the smile of a movie star trapped in a small, lupine frame. "It was inevitable, boss. The machine moves only one way. Forward.

Either you roll with it, or you get rolled underneath. I prefer it on top."

"Spare me the folksy metaphors, Stanley. I've been pulling bloated bodies out of the surf for the past three days, nonstop. And do you know what the worst part about it is? I don't know how many more are going to wash up someplace else tomorrow; under some pier; trapped in some causeway; sucked in through some intake valve. As far as I'm concerned, Stanley, tomorrow can wait. Let the dead bury themselves."

Once, as a young man, Bill O'Gorman had seen a wave of typhoid fever lay waste to an entire section of his hometown in North Jersey, and the local coroner had become a kind of celebrity civil servant, a font of clinical wisdom, quite the hero in a heroless age. So it was with a perverse sense of justice for his hubris at secretly wishing for a typhoid epidemic of his own to overcome, at praying for it, that he was thrust into the maelstrom of the inquest.

The *Slocum* mishap was a political "tar baby." Handled masterfully, it might reward. But, ultimately, if you were identified with it, the pundits intoned, you were marked with death as poignantly as any tar oil marked the hand. A pall would linger over you like a cloud till Judgment Day. And politicians already had enough rough seas to weather. So they bequeathed it to O'Gorman. After all, no city ordinance or statute had been broken. This wasn't a job for the city prosecutor. It was a fire, plain and simple. It called for a coroner's inquest—formal enough to satisfy the critics, yet still four blocks from City Hall, far enough away to keep any distasteful stench at bay.

Most wanted to go after the captain. The fact that he'd traveled ever northward, to North Brother Island, seemed perversely comical in the face of what was happening all around him. His decks had become barbecues, blazing grills, blackened with human flesh. Yet he kept steaming northward.

Others blamed the crew. Ill trained and ill equipped, the Negro deckhands were the easiest targets of all. They had no advocates, no special-interest group. Nobody cared about them, so they served a vital purpose: They marked what no one wanted to be. They were the fringe, the boundary.

And then there were the moneymen, who wanted to target the company. "The line's got the deepest pockets," they were fond of saying. And there was precedent for compensation through awards. A trust fund needed to be set up by the city right away.

Those who combined a lust for legal vengeance with an unbridled hunger for financial punishment, those who craved personal attack while coveting corporate compensation, who thirsted most for justice, claimed that the officers should pay—the members of the Knickerbocker Board. Those who had reaped, or could reap, most of all from the steamboat company's successes were the ones who should be penalized most harshly—Frank A. Barnaby, the president, and his establishment coterie.

And, finally, there were those who wanted to see the country change, to pass new laws, not just to satisfy a sense of justice, but to ensure that this kind of human tragedy would never be performed again. They blamed the U.S. Steamboat Inspection Service—the USSIS. After all, while the *Slocum* had recently passed an inspection, it was clear her lifeboats had been inert, immovable; her hoses ancient and flawed; her life vests decrepit; and, worst, her crew untrained. The USSIS. How quickly this industry acronym became coin of the common realm. Within hours of the disaster, uncounted amateurs changed into instant experts regarding all things maritime, bandying about terms like *USSIS* as if they'd been saying them all their lives. For a few weeks, everyone thought they knew everything.

What did you know, William O'Gorman? I stand beside you, trying to hold you up. Trying to transfer to you whatever it is that keeps me going. Trying to feed your hunger for revenge, or justice—that shining thing inside of you that burns like a living sun.

What did you know as you began to fill out your subpoenas one by one: William Van Schaick, ship's master; Barnaby, Frank A., of the Knickerbocker Steamboat Company; Miss Hall, his secretary; and Henry Lundberg, USSIS inspector. These were the heart and soul of the drama. The crew and passengers were naught but supporting witnesses. It was this ensemble that would help O'Gorman finally understand how something so terrible, and so tactically avoidable, could have transpired in the first place. And on *his* watch. It made a typhoid epidemic seem humdrum.

He gathered up the signed subpoenas. He brandished them in his hand.

Stanley Sikorsky smiled and said, "You won't regret this."

"I regretted it the minute the *Slocum* went down. But you're right, Stanley, as much as I hate to admit it. The machine. It only goes one way."

Stanley Sikorsky skedaddled from the room; he had secured his scrap of wildebeest.

O'Gorman sat at his desk. He found it difficult to move. He sat transfixed. It felt like he'd taken a punch, a sudden uppercut, and he was just too stunned to lie down.

Otto Goldstein hosted a meeting of the Council for German Economic Opportunity, where each month he lost almost twenty-eight dollars entertaining friends, colleagues, and acquaintances, but which rendered dividends immeasurable in power and prestige, which—in turn—could be morphed into money. Goldstein was king in his small kingdom.

The Council met each fortnight at the Golden Rose. It was one of the oldest German business clubs in New York City, boasting in excess of three thousand paying members, and twice that many aspirants. The top twenty-five officers, the richest men in Kleindeutschland, made up the Council. Every major delicatessen, each lumber company and hardware store, each beer garden of significance, each haberdashery of note, each bakery and slaughterhouse, was represented in this room.

They sat around the table in the Golden Rose's most lavish private dining room. They were debating the defection of many of their members to the growing ranks of Socialist Workers' Clubs. The entire next generation of councilmen was growing up reading Marx.

"We must do something," Hans Schulman Bering said. "I've lost my two best managers." Tall and willowy, Bering looked like a Prussian colonel, with boisterous mustaches that seemed to be fighting to the death immediately below his nose. Bering owned nearly all the stockyards and slaughterhouses of Kleindeutschland, plus a bank.

"You fired them," the laconic Pieter Max replied. Max owned all the fish stores and most of the fish wholesalers in the district. He was short and squat, with the chilling poise and patience of an octopus.

"Well, I had to. They spread talk about collective bargaining, of unions and the like. What was I meant to do? How do you manage it, Otto?" Bering asked.

Goldstein took a long draft of pale ale. He put his stein down on the table and wiped his mouth with the back of his hand. He waited another moment and said, "Excuse me? What did you say? Manage what exactly, Hans?"

The pause would have been enough to ward off most inquisitors. But Bering would not be assuaged. This issue of the workers' clubs was like a burr under his saddle. "Your *Meister Brauer*, Arvin. He runs the People's Union."

"I believe that Leonard Meer is chairman of that club."

"You know what I mean, Goldstein. Meer may be chairman, but we all know who's in charge. If he hadn't been born a Jew . . . Anyway, how do you keep your master brewer in line?"

"Arvin Brauer?" said Max. "The father of Dustin Brauer, no?"

"The same," said Bering. His sparkling light blue eyes grew wide. He had found reinforcements.

"What will you do about Dustin?" said Pieter Max with a frown.

"I thought we were talking about the workers' clubs."

"We've been dancing about this all night," Max replied. He spoke with uncharacteristic candor. He slammed his stein on the table. "Ernest, Derek, Bruno. Herman, Kiefer, and Kurt. You lost your wives. Otis and Roland. Rudolph and Willis. You lost daughters." He turned with a sneer upon Goldstein. "I lost two daughters, my eldest son, and Gretchen, my wife. Otto, you lost your Ula. We've just spent almost two hours talking about charities and rehabilitation funds. We've touched on everything—from coffins to insurance collateral. We've even gone through our obligatory moaning about the blasted workers' clubs . . . again. As we do each fortnight. No one has said it, so I will. What about this Dustin Brauer? What are we going to do? Or are we to think our chairman is so concerned, so worried about losing his master brewer, that he'd rather cover his eyes to the truth? The inevitable. The indisputable. Someone must pay, Otto, someone. The people demand it. Someone was responsible, and someone has to pay."

"I believe that's what the coroner's inquest is about," said Goldstein flatly. He could feel the eyes of everyone in the room. They were burning a hole in his head, his neck and back. He felt like an insect, like one of those cockroaches he used to set on fire with his magnifying glass as a boy.

"The coroner's inquest!" Kiefer Munch began to laugh. Gnomelike and bald, and dressed in a plain black suit, it was hard to believe Munch ran the largest haberdashery in Kleindeutschland. "You think our families care about the inquest? Our women—those who survived, that is; those who remain—all know it's a farce. Frank Barnaby will never serve a day in jail, mark my words. Neither will Lundberg. The city will protect them. But who will protect us, if not this Council? Let them have their public inquest. They'll crucify the captain and sweep the rest away, like so much trash, under the city rug."

"He's right," said Bering.

"We cannot duck this," Max said blithely. "What do we do about Dustin?"

"The fact my master brewer is his father is irrelevant. But I need to stand aside," said Goldstein, waving a hand. "I have to, gentlemen. Don't you see? The only one who's accused Dustin of anything is my own son. And, to be frank—"

"Don't say it, Otto," Bering said.

"Say what?" Goldstein answered with frustration. "How can I say anything when you keep interrupting me?"

"Let him speak," said Max.

"My son," said Goldstein with a nod to Max. "How can I put this? Well, he's not always been one hundred percent honest with me. There. Are you happy, Hans?" he said to Bering.

"Are you?"

"This bickering is pointless," Munch said. "We have to act. Kleindeutschland demands it. Where is this boy?"

"I don't know," said Goldstein.

"How can you not know? He's your master brewer's son. Ask Arvin; he's here someplace. I saw him earlier," said Max.

Goldstein sighed. He whispered an order to one of his servants, and he returned, minutes later, with Arvin Brauer in tow.

"You called for me, Herr Goldstein?" Arvin said with a smile, wiping his hands on his apron.

Arvin was the finest brewer he had ever known. Goldstein hung his head. "You know what my son has been saying?"

"Yes, Herr Goldstein. About Dustin. But it's not true, sir, I swear it. My son didn't do it. It wasn't his cigarette—"

Goldstein raised his hand. "That may be so. But, until we know, until we're absolutely sure, we're bound to harvest the truth, isn't that right, Arvin? Honor bound. Make no mistake. There will be an inquest. A Kleindeutschland inquest. There are facts here which need to be uncovered."

"A Kleindeutschland pogrom, you mean, sir."

"Be careful, Herr Brauer. Please don't make this about your faith."

"What facts?"

"Where's your son?" Pieter Max said. "He's not at his job. Leonard Meer hasn't seen him all day."

"I don't know. Is he falling behind in his work?"

"What do you mean, you don't know?" Goldstein said. "He lives in your house, does he not?"

"Not a house, sir. The Delancey Gardens. Quite modest, really."

"Does he live there or not?"

"Last night," Arvin said, "Dustin never came home. He must be staying with friends."

"What friends?" Bering asked.

"I don't know."

"In Kleindeutschland?" added Max.

"I don't know."

There was a collective sigh. Everyone looked back at Goldstein. He shrugged and took another sip of his ale. There were too many options, he thought. Inconclusive and vague. Too many pieces on the chessboard. "Well," he said. "See to it that you inform me immediately, as soon as your son returns home."

"Of course, Herr Goldstein," Arvin answered with a small bow. He backed his way out of the crowd, away from the table. He scurried through the door and was gone.

"He'll never tell you," Hans Bering continued. "Just like my general managers. I bet he's laughing at you right now, as we speak, behind your back. He knows where his son is. You think he doesn't? He just isn't telling you." Bering sucked on his stein. "This is how it always starts. Always the same," he bemoaned. "How many more members do you think we'll lose to workers' clubs if we let Arvin Brauer thumb his nose at us? How many, Otto? We must do something."

"Draw a line," said Max. "As Bismarck did with the socialists at home. Mark a boundary."

"You said it yourself," added Keifer. "Let them have their inquest, and Kleindeutschland will have hers. Do we deserve less? Otto, you must call it."

"But my son—"

"I lost *my* son," Max cut in. "He burned to death on the deck of that ship. But I'm not thinking of him, or of my wife, or of my daughters who burned there beside him. And certainly not of myself. I'm thinking of this Council. Bering is right. It is your duty, Otto, as chairman. It is your obligation."

And so it was. Goldstein hung his head. He thought and thought, but nothing came. The outcome of Kleindeutschland's inquest was irrelevant. He'd lost already. "Very well," he said. "But, since my son is involved, and since I will not preside over anything that smacks of bias, I call for an investigating board. All of you. Each one of you, who seems to care so much, must be provided with a way, a means to defend your interests. A voice, if you will."

"In other words," said Pieter Max, "if you burn, you want company."

And they sat there and deliberated. I watched them orchestrate the future. I watched them cogitate and strategize, conduct scenario planning, whine and prognosticate, and finally define. By the time it was over, everyone was on the hook for something. Goldstein had seen to that. Although it brought him little comfort.

He sat by himself in his private dining room later that night, curled like a question mark by the fire. He sat there and stared at the flames. There had been no way to counter, no way to deflect or respond. As soon as Bingham had opened his mouth, the game was already complete. Finished. Kaput. Checkmate. The workers' unions and collectives and clubs. These were mere frosting. The cake was Arvin Brauer. The man who held the key to Goldstein's personal treasury. The brewer of the Golden Rose's most infamous pale ale. Otto had nothing. He didn't even own the beer garden. He'd ceded the deed to Ula on their wedding day. And then that ghost, that ancient ragged specter, crawled back into view. Arvin Brauer and Ula Goldstein. What a couple they made. They were the ones who ran things anyway, or so everyone believed. Arvin and Ula. Ula and Arvin. Goldstein watched the old fears prancing in his head. Ula and Arvin, that time in the kitchen. That awkward pregnant pause. Arvin and Ula, descending the stairs. Her laughter, that giggle, delightful as church chimes, which ceased just as Otto approached. Ula and Arvin by the kegs in the basement, managing assets. That Jew! There was a will somewhere; someplace, there was, Otto knew. Ula had drafted one right after Heinemann's death. That Jew was probably in it. He was probably her beneficiary. Ula owned the tavern. Arvin, the recipe. And Otto . . . Yes, what did Otto own? Who was he but the crack where two great fortunes converged, the space in between, a strand for the land and the sea?

It hurts to be in Otto Goldstein. So why do I return? It stings. It stings.

Or Bingham might be beneficiary. He was her son, after all— Ula's natural heir. And then the deepest fear of all: But who was Bingham's father?

Let me go.

CHAPTER 8

June 20, 1904

New York City

The gallery was crowded with people. All of the hot summer air in the chambers seemed to have coalesced near the ceiling, confounding their minds, making them dizzy. They could barely move. They could barely breathe, it was so humid. And the inquest started late.

The chambers were modest. Citizens of greater influence and representatives of the press sat together on the main floor below. There were so many small tables and chairs that it was hard to maneuver through the room. The coroner, or the manager of the coroner's office, Stanley Sikorsky, presided over the events from a raised platform at the head of the chambers. A serious young man, with long muttonchop sideburns, sat beside him—the official recorder. Throughout the trial, he never changed his suit. And at the edge of the platform, by the coroner's table, sat the witness. The jury had been corralled into a narrow wooden frame made of pine by the dais. Ten gentlemen sat, while five more stood behind, in reserve.

And it occurred to me, as I looked down, that except for a witness occasionally, all on the main floor were men. Such a thing would never have preoccupied me previously. How strange that in my sexless incorporeal state, it should become so glaringly apparent. Perhaps that's why. Perhaps you have to be outside of sex to see it.

I watched my mother and my father watching. I watched them through Louisa's eyes. She sat on the edge of her seat, craning her neck for a superior view of the gallery. We knew all the families: Otto and Bingham Goldstein; the willowy Hans Bering; Kiefer Munch; and Pieter Max; and Herr Brauer, sitting off to the side. But Dustin was nowhere to be seen. Dustin was hiding.

Then came the parade—all the witnesses. After a while, the memories began to merge, to blend and overlap. In truth, the people all began to sound alike. They all began to sound like me.

"I saw the crew at the fire hose," said the woman. She was fifty and fat and wore far too much rouge.

"And did they turn it on? The hose. Did they turn on the water?" asked the coroner.

"I don't think they knew how. Finally, a white officer came out and turned it on. That's when the hose burst. It was too old. I suppose it couldn't stand the pressure."

And then: "The lifeboats weren't lashed to the deck. I know somebody said that before. One of your other witnesses. That isn't true," said the man.

"Are you sure?" said the coroner.

"Much worse." He was a former naval officer, a man with some experience.

"What could be worse?"

"The brackets were rusted. Frankly, I doubt that they'd ever been used. And the bolts; they were falling apart. They were oxidized."

"Rusted?"

"Yes, through and through, sir. The bolts and the washers were fused. The lifeboats, all of them, weren't lashed to the deck . . . except, perhaps, by neglect."

And then: "It was chaos," said a woman. "It was hell." She wore a spring bonnet with flowers. "I witnessed a wave of small children descending. The clothes on their backs were on fire. And they screamed." She brought a lace kerchief to her face, blew her nose. She took another deep breath. "I watched them jump into the water. There was a little opening behind one of the lifeboats, and they entered it one by one. Then they jumped. Some hesitated, afraid—I suppose—when they got a good view of the water. But they were pushed by the crowd nonetheless. I watched them fall into the river, still blazing. I watched as they floated and bobbed, as they slipped through the waves. All of them. One by one. There must have been fifteen or twenty. One by one, they all drowned."

"And how old were these children?" asked the coroner.

"Three or four. I doubt any were older than five. Some were younger." She paused. "They looked like they'd just learned how to walk."

By the late afternoon, I had wearied of words. My father had gone back to work. My mother still sat there, still worrying her gown. And Louisa—she languished beside her, her cheek to her forearm. I could feel the moisture where her skin touched the wood of the rail. She was tired. She hadn't slept in a week. Perhaps it was my own I was thinking of, as I reached out reflexively, and pressed my fingers to her eyes. I could not close my eyes. I had no eyelids left to close.

But my fingers, they slithered right through her. So I reached out again. Again, and again. I imagined her eyelids, the soft ivory skin. I imagined them kissing my fingertips. I could picture it, and they closed. They closed!

"We call William Van Schaick."

And Louisa woke up. She straightened and stretched, leaned forward and peered down at the seaman who was mounting the dais. Captain William Van Schaick was a slight man, narrow-shouldered, with delicate features offset by a bushy mustache. Handlebar. He had translucent eyes, hazel-colored. Or eye. For the other still carried a bandage, where an ember had flown in and damaged the pupil. He made his way up the small steps. He laid his left hand on the Bible and brought the other aloft.

"Do you solemnly swear . . ."

And he did. He sat on the chair. He took off his cap. He gathered the room up, the faces. The way the audience looked at him, he would remember their eyes for the rest of his life. Perhaps longer. He curled a thumb in his collar. The material was pinching his skin. His lapels were drawn tight at the neck. His uniform, double-breasted and wool, was buttoned from nipple to navel. It was hot in the courtroom, and by the time he had settled, his forehead was covered in sweat.

"You've been captain of the *General Slocum* steamboat for how long, Captain Van Schaick?"

"Since she was launched—'91. Thirteen years."

"And isn't it true that the unfortunate event which transpired last week was not the first time the *Slocum*'s been . . . how should I put this?" the coroner said. "Damaged?"

"No, sir," Van Schaick replied.

"How many times?"

"How many times what, sir?"

"How many incidents, accidents, whatever you wish to call them? How many has the *Slocum* suffered since she was launched?"

"In August of our first year of operation, there was two accidents: She ran aground in Rockaway on the fourteenth and, three days later, backed into another steamer."

"Is that it?"

"No. Seven years later, on July ninth, '98, to be exact, she rammed the *Amelia* near the Battery. Then, in 1902, she ran aground at low tide on a sandbar in Jamaica Bay—while trying to avoid hitting a yacht, I might add. And she bumped another party boat as the two tried docking at the same pier two months later."

"Is that it?"

"Traffic accidents . . ."

"What's that? Did you say something, Captain?"

"No."

"I'm sure I heard you say something. Come now, Captain. Don't be coy. What did you say?"

"I said 'traffic accidents.' That's all that they were, those events. With any working ship, these kinds of things happen."

"Well, I would hardly characterize the death of more than a thousand innocent men, women, and children a 'traffic accident.' I would venture to guess the survivors of the *Slocum*—many of whom are with us here today—don't care to recall what transpired in precisely that way."

"That's not what I meant," said Van Schaick. His eye rolled about in his head.

"I'm sure," said the coroner. "Captain Van Schaick. Tell us, then, in your own words, what happened last week. From the beginning."

The captain composed himself. He sat back in the witness chair. He looked at the crowd. Well, not quite *at* the crowd. In truth, he looked *above* the crowd, over their heads, at the long blank wall behind them, at the door, the invisible hallway, the street, and the quickest way back to the sea.

"We set sail in the morning. Locust Grove was our heading.

And, at first, everything went smoothly. As it always did. It was the end of the Sunday-school year, and we had a large group of passengers from St. Mark's. There was music and singing and dancing. It was . . . beautiful. But in less than an hour, as we passed through Hell Gate, right across from Astoria Park . . ."

And I heard the waltzes again. I saw people still dancing in the soft morning light. They were laughing and singing and planning their outings. They were already ashore in their minds.

"The fire began in the Lamp Room. There's no doubt about that," said Van Schaick. "How, we're uncertain. A careless cigarette, perhaps. Or a match. We'll probably never know. A box of straw caught on fire, and the fire spread. The *Slocum*. She's a fine . . . she *was* a fine ship. I was proud to command her. She was built by Devine-Burtis of Brooklyn, at the height of the market. But the way the stairwells were designed, they served as chimneys to the fire. They drew the flames aloft."

"How long before you knew about the fire?"

"It took several minutes. Perhaps as many as ten . . ."

"Ten minutes!"

"The fire had to be discovered. And then the men spent several minutes trying to put it out. But they failed. The fire spread."

"And why, when you found out about the blaze, didn't you put in somewhere—Manhattan or Queens? Why keep on sailing to North Brother Island?"

"The shore was busy with oil tanks. I feared a secondary blaze."

"A secondary blaze."

"That's right. The last thing I wanted to do was steer the burning *Slocum* into an oil depot. North Brother Island was just a mile away."

"I'd venture to guess that a mile seemed like a long way away to the people burning each and every second on your decks."

"Hundreds survived. None would have if I'd brought her to shore by the oil tanks."

"Is that an expert opinion? Are you trained in the forensics of fire?"

"No, sir," Van Schaick said, gritting his teeth. "But I've been a licensed captain for almost twenty years. And I was there. Don't forget. I was there. I'd probably do the same thing again, if faced with the same situation."

"Probably. Please continue your story." William O'Gorman leaned forward. He looked fascinated.

Captain Van Schaick swallowed hard. It was a gesture so painful we could see it from the gallery. He started and stopped. He breathed and he said, "By the time we got to North Brother, the vessel was lost. The fire had spread. Each deck was ablaze. I ordered the lifeboats be lowered. I told them to hand out the vests." He smiled grimly. "The life vests."

"What about them?"

"I knew they were in need of replacement. I'd been complaining to the company for months."

"You'd requested new life vests from Knickerbocker?"

"On more than one occasion."

"Go on."

"But the fire . . . The fire just kept coming. There was no time for anything. So I beached her."

"On North Brother Island."

"Yes, sir. I beached her so the passengers could try and get ashore, away from the fire. Many had jumped already, but more still crowded the decks. There's a contagious-disease hospital on the island, currently being renovated. Nurses and patients came running out to assist us. They brought ladders from the renovation. They used them to bring people ashore. Some caught babies in their arms, thrown down from the decks. Many were burning. The babies. I saw things . . . things that no man should see." He paused and looked out at the crowd. "When it was clear she was done for, me and my crew went below. There was naught we could do any longer. Somehow, we made it to the ladders. The smoke was very thick. And the smell . . . I remember sitting on the rail, my foot tucked in a scupper, looking back at the pilothouse. I remember hearing the decks. They uttered a great groan, then a wail, and gave way. I saw flames shoot up from the holds. She just broke apart. Just . . . broke, like a toy. Her decks split and I saw people shower down into the opening. It was grotesque. All of those arms and legs and bodies tumbling down. Into the heart of the inferno. As if a crack had opened up in the earth, like a doorway to hell. I'll never forget it, as long as I live. I'll never forget."

"Is that when you abandoned the ship?"

The captain looked up. There were tears in his one cyclops eye. "Yes, sir," he said. His voice was emotionless, dead. Talking seemed pointless. There were not enough sentences, enough words in the world left to cover the truth. He shrugged once and said, "Then we ran."

CHAPTER 9

June 20, 1904
New York City

The Kleindeutschland inquest convened at the Rose. The people—they gathered, in packs, based on family, friendship, or some other affinity; on the clan of their commerce; their kind. They fused into clumps, like the cells of a tumor.

Goldstein presided over the inquest, flanked by Kiefer Munch, Hans Bering, and Pieter Max. Arvin Brauer sat off to the side. There was much discussion at the start about rules, codes of conduct, about honor and moral obedience. And then, when the crowd finally settled, when their knees had stopped wiggling and their ankles had stilled, Otto Goldstein called Bingham, his son.

The boy entered the room through the back. He was suddenly there. He was dressed in a uniform—the dark navy blazer and shorts preferred by the priests at St. Mark's. His wavy black hair was well oiled and slicked back, combed and coiffed but seemingly tensile, like a very slow liquid, like glass. He moved to the chair by the dais; a stout set of beer crates, all jumbled together. He sat. He looked at the crowd. Then he started his story. He had told it so many times now that the words seemed nonsensical. He was sick of them now. His mouth had shaped them too often.

The story poured out, and I noticed, as I sat in the corner alone, that Bingham never leaned back. He sat stiff as a pikestaff. He unrolled his soliloquy slowly. He tugged at the narrative, first gumming the words, then disgorging them into the crowd—like a heron from Schlüsselburg feeding its young. He looked as though he were sleepwalking. Goldstein had fed him a spoonful of laudanum, a few drops, after breakfast. It wiggled just under the skin

But Karl Lehman and Abelard Warner were different. Skinny Karl fairly quivered. Like most cowards, he was a scavenger, more at ease with the lifeless, the sick, or the wounded. He had never been under the eye of so large a convention, and he stuttered repeatedly, mumbling his speech.

" . . . the fire burst out of the fo'c'sle," he said.

"The Lamp Room," said Goldstein. It was the fourth time he'd corrected the boy.

"The Lamp Room. Yes. Of course."

"Please, go on."

"Where Brauer had entered before."

"Moments earlier."

"Moments earlier."

I don't know if it was the narrative or the coaching that I resented the most. Their manner of speaking was practiced, rehearsed, each phrase and each sentence scripted. But the story lacked color. It was imprisoned by facts. It bobbled and bounced noun to noun, badly cabled by verbs, like a johnboat in difficult seas. He was finally excused.

Fat Abelard was startlingly different. His memory of the script had been swamped by his own recollections. Try as he might, he wasn't able to silence the screaming, nor muffle the shuffle of desperate feet, the scratching of nail against wall. That smell, he couldn't suppress it, of the people who had herded together, trapped like rats, with that bulkhead still blocking their freedom. The fire crept up on them slowly, singeing their backs, as they scratched at the bulkhead. *Scratch. Scratch.* Till it stopped.

"You saw Dustin enter the Lamp Room?" asked Goldstein.

"Yes, I did. We all did. Not just me, but Bingham and Karl Lehman, too."

"Then what happened?"

"He lit up a cigarette. Mallory Meer had just left. He was smoking alone. By himself. In the dark. The Lamp Room was below the main deck, toward the bow."

"But if it was dark in the Lamp Room, how could you see?"

Abelard paused on a memory. His eyes rolled; he furrowed his brow. He looked like a newly hooked fish. Then he said, "When he smoked, as he puffed, the ember grew bright. It lit up his face. We could see him." He paused and glanced out at the crowd. "Then he finished his cigarette. He flicked it away. It rolled on the planking."

"Be specific," said Goldstein. "Try to focus. Where did it roll?" he continued.

"To that box full of straw."

"And Dustin Brauer, what of him?"

"He stepped from the Lamp Room. He never looked back. He just turned and headed away."

"I see," Goldstein said. "He went topside, aloft?"

"He just left."

"Now—and this is important. Abelard. Abelard, are you listening?"

The boy was trapped in his reverie. He was looking within.

"Abelard!"

"Yes, sir," he said. "Yes, Herr Goldstein."

"Did you see that box catch on fire? Did you actually see it ignite?"

"Yes, Herr Goldstein. I did."

"That's a lie," Arvin said from the corner. A wave of disdain swept the room.

"Silence," said Goldstein. "Or I'll have you removed. Just be quiet," he added, now softening. He twisted his body, looking down on his brewer. "You'll have your opportunity to speak, Herr Brauer. All in good time." He looked back at Fat Abelard.

The boy seemed to melt in his seat. His suit was too small for him—it had belonged to his less corpulent brother—and the skin of his neck pillowed over like lava. The jowls of his face gently quivered. His eyes bulged; his lips pursed. His head seemed no longer attached. It looked like his neck had been broken. He looked, strangely, like a hanged man.

"Abelard Warner. You know the difference between lying and telling the truth. You heard Lehman testify earlier. Karl said he was certain . . . one hundred percent certain: It was Dustin Brauer's cigarette that set fire to that box. Can you corroborate his statement?"

"Can I do what?"

"Is that what happened?" Goldstein asked. "Dustin Brauer threw his cigarette to the deck. Then he turned and walked away, without once looking back to make sure. He simply headed down the passageway. And, climbing aloft, ventured out onto the deck—the busy promenade, I believe—where he stopped. Where he waited and waited until the cigarette had done its work.

"Who can say what he thought, as he waited there, safe, by the rail? Abelard, do you know? *Can* you know? Who can say what dream burned in his head as the fire grew larger below?

"Perhaps this was not a planned venture. Perhaps it was just reckless abandon, a misfortunate oversight, deadly fun. But as unpremeditated as the act may have been, the result was the same." Goldstein shook his round head. "The cigarette Dustin Brauer rolled, smoked, and then tossed without a moment's hesitation to the floor killed more than a thousand men, women, and children. Burned them. And drowned them. Our sisters and daughters. Our wives. Lest we forget, in a moment of tenderness, as we look on the face of a child. Lest we forget."

Goldstein swiveled and stared down at Fat Abelard. The boy squirmed in his seat. "One more thing, Abelard, if you don't mind. Do you know what happened to Dustin Brauer once the fire grew out of control?"

"Yes, Herr Goldstein. We followed him topside, as you said. We didn't know the fire was out of control when we left. We thought it was just a small blaze. Anyway, we climbed the stairwell and came upon him on deck. On the promenade. He was leaning against the port rail. When the fire grew out of control, he was one of the first to abandon the steamboat. Somehow, someway, he made it across to a tugboat astern."

"What do you mean, somehow managed? Either he crossed or he didn't."

"Yes, he did, sir."

"And he was safe and out of danger, out of harm's way, well before the *Slocum* was lost; isn't that true?"

"Yes, Herr Goldstein."

"A quite miraculous escape, wouldn't you say?"

"Yes, sir. It couldn't have been better planned. I mean, *if* it were planned. I know I can't comment on that—to intent."

Arvin Brauer got up from his seat. He glared up at Goldstein. "That's enough," he said tightly. "You call this justice? This is a farce, nothing more. A charade."

An undertow of grumbling clutched at the room. The dining hall hummed with dissent. "Sit down," someone said. "Dirty Jew."

"I've not called you yet, Arvin," said Goldstein. "Please do me the courtesy of taking your seat."

"I will not, and you cannot compel me. Not as a judge. And not as my employer, either. Not any longer," he said. "I'm through, done with the Rose and this neighborhood." He trembled as he spoke. He was afraid yet transfixed, lit up by some bright inner light. "Shame on you, all of you," he continued. "Shame on your bigotry. Your spiteful guilt. Your hunger for revenge. Shame on you all. I tell you—may the dead come back to haunt me, if I'm wrong—these boys are lying. My son is innocent. He has done nothing to warrant your hatred. He's not even here to defend himself, to face his accusers—"

"Exactly," said Goldstein. "Where is he? Why isn't he here, if he's innocent?"

"Where do you think he is? He's hiding from this mob. Hiding from you. Where else could he be?"

"You give me no choice, Arvin Brauer. If you don't produce your son by sundown tomorrow, it is *you* we'll hand over. To the authorities. To the police. Do you hear me, Herr Brauer? The witnesses were clear, their testimony unimpeachable. Your son, Dustin Brauer, started that fire, which resulted in uncounted dead. You've made yourself his accomplice, an accessory to murder. It is *you* who is guilty," he added, washing his hands in the air.

Arvin moved toward the exit.

"You have not been excused," Goldstein said. "Do you hear me? Arvin Brauer? Arvin Brauer, sit down!" He nodded almost imperceptibly, and two men with muttonchops appeared by the door.

Arvin hesitated. His eyes darted about the dining hall, but there was no ready exit. The two men approached him. Arvin stood still as they hooked their arms around his elbows. "Yes, I can hear you," he said. "It's all very clear now, Herr Goldstein." A frightful smile played on his lips. They started to lead him away. "As long as you've got your scapegoat, what does it matter?" he shouted. "What do you care, any of you? One Jew's as good as another."

I came to Dustin in a dream. He lay on the floor, at the foot of the bed of his friend Henrik Silverstein. It was the first time he had slept in three days. He was curled in a blanket, still dressed in his work clothes and boots.

He was dreaming of tropical islands, of palm-fronded atolls and bright turquoise seas. He listened to seabirds: shrill gulls, raucous terns. He savored the salt in the spray. At first I was loath to disturb him. He slumbered so peacefully. He was so far away. But the wolves of Kleindeutschland were circling. They had visited all of his family, and most of his friends in the district already.

Tall and slender, like Dustin, but with curly brown hair, Henrik lived on Fourteenth Street, between Eighth and Ninth. He was an only child. His mother worked as housekeeper to a retired sea captain. They shared two rooms at the top of a wonderful five-story brownstone. The floors had been pilfered from ship decks—the stoutest of strakes, hand-fitted and practically seamless. The main floor was checkered with marble—*crema marfil* from Carrara in Italy. A huge gilded mirror from Marseille graced the foyer. And the railing from Juneau was so perfectly jointed that it looked to be carved from one tree. Henrik's father had gone to work one morning and never returned. There were times when Henrik imagined him walking the streets of these strange far-off cities, the wellspring of each wondrous thing in the house.

The servants' quarters were a great deal more humble, of course. But to Dustin, the size of the rooms, their airiness, and that skylight that blistered with sunlight on most afternoons in the summer made the Silverstein home seem like paradise.

I was loath to disturb him . . . but I did. One minute he was hauling wind, bearing down on a following sea, and the next he stood beside Barnaby, in the offices of the Knickerbocker Steamboat Company. Miss Hall hovered close by. I could sense Dustin's wonder. I could feel his confusion unfurl. He knew nothing of these people, and yet they seemed real. He felt as though he should know them.

"Yes, Mr. Barnaby. As you wish, sir," Miss Hall said. "Life jackets were already on order."

Dustin awoke. He glanced about the darkened room. It was almost 2:00 A.M. Henrik was sleeping, his breathing soft and profound. Gaslight played on the ceiling. Somewhere a man coughed on Fourteenth Street below. A horse neighed. A girl laughed. Dustin tried to sit up. He tried to roll, but his arms and his legs were immobile. *Mr. Barnaby,* he thought. He knew that name! It had been splashed across the front page of every newspaper in the city for a week. Frank Barnaby, of the Knickerbocker Steamboat Company. *Life jackets were already on order.* But what did it mean?

The hairs on the back of his neck stood on end. Someone was there; he could sense it. Someone or something. Right there! A cold wind swept through him. He tried to get up but he couldn't. He was frozen with fear. He was paralyzed. A dog howled in the distance.

"Dustin?" said Henrik. He stirred and looked over the bed. "Dustin, are you all right? You're pale as a sheet."

Dustin closed his eyes, then opened them again. His mouth was dry as dead leaves. Slowly but surely, the blood returned to his veins.

"It's nothing," he said. And then, like a nail through my heart: "Just a dream."

Chapter 10

June 21, 1904
New York City

Henry Lundberg winked at his fiancée as he mounted the dais. He was dressed in a worsted wool suit trimmed with velvet. His luxurious lead-colored tie matched his army gray shirt with precision, setting off his bright violet eyes. His shiny black hair—the envy of many a girl—rolled off his shoulders in waves. His eyebrows were plucked, his cheeks naturally rouged. He unbuttoned a button and sat.

Stanley Sikorsky had been responsible for presiding over the inquest all morning, interviewing lesser personages. O'Gorman arrived fairly late. He seemed out of sorts and impatient—*verklempt*, as Dustin would say. Despite the fact that the inquest had been running quite smoothly, the coroner was taking his lumps in the press. The process was taking too long. The interviews weren't thorough enough, or they suffered from length, or from brevity, or from an overabundance of facts. They were either too sharp or too pasty, like a fruit that's never in season. They were nobody's favorite.

"You are an inspector for the United States Steamboat Inspection Service—the USSIS—are you not?" said O'Gorman.

"I'm privileged to serve in the Service."

O'Gorman looked down at the witness. "Just answer the question, please."

"I am."

"And you were responsible for inspecting the *General Slocum*, correct?"

"I am but one of many, sir, serving in the Service, who've been blessed to inspect, or to otherwise make an inspection of, the *General Slocum*, to be sure."

"A *yes* or a *no* will do fine, thank you."

"Most certainly. Yes."

"And did you, or did you not conduct an inspection of the *Slocum* on March seventeenth of this year, on behalf of the USSIS?"

"I would hesitate to say it was on behalf of the Service. I am, it is true, an employee. But—and do not think me self-serving—I prefer to think of myself as *being* the Service, if you know what I mean, when in service . . . to the Service." He gave O'Gorman a wink.

This final gesture seemed to set O'Gorman off. "Just answer the questions, damn you."

Henry Lundberg looked appalled. He wilted in his seat. "I beg your pardon, Coroner," he said.

"I apologize, Inspector Lundberg. For cursing. But please stick to the facts. And only to the facts. I'm sure your opinions and feelings and intuitions and kinesthetic sensations are of great and vital importance to you, but they don't serve the needs of this inquest. Now, if you'd do me the honor of answering my questions with simple replies—say, a *yes* or a *no,* I'm sure we'd all greatly appreciate it. Perhaps, then, we'll be able to get off to lunch at a reasonable hour, for a change."

It was hot in the chambers. A fly settled on Louisa's arm, and she shook it away.

"By all means," Lundberg said.

I looked down upon his fiancée, Mabel Smith. But all I could see was that picture Lundberg kept in his head. With her skirt up, that thigh.

"When you made your inspection, did you find the life vests in working order?"

"Well, you see, sir. It's difficult to remember exactly what I thought about them."

"It's only been three months."

"Three months to you, sir, but sixteen steamships, twenty-four schooners, and thirteen assorted smaller vessels to me. I did, however, review my personal diary this morning. Based on my entry of March seventeenth, it's clear, without doubt, that I gathered the life vests were in satisfactory condition."

"Satisfactory?"

"As I said."

"And were you aware that, according to his testimony, Captain Van Schaick had requested new life vests from the Knickerbocker Steamboat Company on more than one occasion?"

"I was not. If that's true."

"Do you have any reason to believe that it's not true?"

"Well, sir. And I say this with the utmost respect. A man like Captain Van Schaick, in his position, as it were, as the master of a ship that went down . . . well, I naturally question his view of events. A sunk ship does funny things to a captain. I've seen it before, many times. Funny things."

"Funny things," O'Gorman repeated, looking out at the crowd. Somebody laughed. Then somebody else, who followed another, and soon the whole room was guffawing. But I couldn't laugh, though I wanted to. It just didn't come.

"And what, Mr. Lundberg, did you think of the lifeboats? Were they locked into place? Were they worthless?"

"Well, sir, *worthless* is a difficult term. In the hands of expert seamen, few things are worthless. Why, I've seen men whittle keys out of nothing but pieces of seashell. My diary, which I keep with punctilious care, mind you, tells me: 'the lifeboats were painted and seaworthy.'"

"Painted and seaworthy, perhaps. But worthless if lashed to the deck. If the hinges were fused, full of rust, Mr. Lundberg."

"Well, there you are, sir. That's what I mean. Rust is a curious thing. It can enter the tiniest places, at the most inopportune time. Especially when metal's exposed to the sea. 'Salt slays,' as they say."

"Do they really? And the hoses. More than twenty eyewitnesses said that they burst. They were rotten, Mr. Lundberg. The pressure simply destroyed them."

"Yes, I heard that. Once again, sir. As an expert in these sorts of things, I can attest, firsthand, what the sea air can do to the stoutest material. Why, in no time at all, sailcloth can shred, hinges can rust, hoses can crumble. Mother Nature, you know, can be the cruelest of mistresses."

"Frankly, Mr. Lundberg—and I say this 'with the utmost respect'—your inspection of the *Slocum* was cursory at best. Others have testified that you were aboard the steamboat for less than ten minutes. *Ten minutes*, Mr. Lundberg. Hardly enough time to share a pint with the captain, which, we have heard from Van Schaick, you apparently did. A pint of ale, while on duty. I'm shocked, Mr. Lundberg."

The crowd burst into laughter.

O'Gorman held up his hand. "Is this true, Mr. Lundberg?"

"It is customary for the master of a vessel to offer the inspector on service a beverage. It's tradition."

"Tradition! Tradition, sir, is honoring your sworn duty. Tradition's ensuring that what you're inspecting passes muster. It's making sure that those innocent children had a chance. Do we, in this city, in this country, actually care about public safety? Does the USSIS really matter?"

"I beg your pardon, sir, Coroner O'Gorman, but do you have any idea how many steamboats and ships, how many coasters and tugboats and barges and barks, how many schooners and sloops we inspect every year? Do you have any idea?"

"No. How many?"

"Well, I'm not exactly sure what the number is, but it's in the hundreds of thousands, in all forty-five states. To be sure, sir, as you see, we're not idle."

"No," said O'Gorman. He threw Lundberg a withering gaze. "I'm sure it must take serious effort to ascend to such dizzying heights of incompetence. Please, Mr. Lundberg, lest I tax you further. Please, sir." He motioned. "Step down."

Abelard slept in his bed, with his four older brothers, and a sister. It was a large bed, for the Warners were stout.

Abelard was dreaming of whales. He was master harpooner on a ship from Point Barrow, well out on the cold Bering Sea. It had been but forty years since "Seward's Folly," when Secretary of State William Seward had handed Edouard de Stoeckl, Russian minister, a check for $7 million in exchange for Alaska. The territory was still as foreign to Abelard as Minn-e-so-ta had been to Arvin Brauer.

He rode on the prow of the ship, his bright harpoon ready. In his dream, he was svelte. And the whale—she ascended, undaunted, before him. She climbed and he threw, and I forced him to pass through his quarry, to become her, as I slipped on his skin like a glove, like a meat puppet. He woke up. He could feel me already. And he wondered—how strange—how his brothers could sleep. They snored and they whistled around him. Nothing could stir them. They slept like the dead.

It was *his* face I cradled in my hands, that first time. Not my love's. It was Abelard's face. I touched him, and he flinched, quite repulsed, and his heart seemed to leap from his chest. He sat up. He grew pale. He grew cold. Very cold. Was it this, or his fear, at the root of his chattering teeth? Was it me or his guilt? *This,* I thought as I stroked him.

"Who's there," he cried out. "Show yourself."

No, Abelard. You don't want to see me. That I promise you. Not as I really am—bloated and armless, and ravaged by crabs.

"Come out, I say." He sat up. He was bare-chested and his milkless breast muscles jiggled and sagged. His hair stood up on its ends. Goose bumps popped out on his shoulders and neck. He was speechless. He had lost all his words. So I uttered two up through his throat. I just pushed them. "The truth," he exclaimed. And again. "The truth." As I held his round face in my fingers.

And it burned. It burned.

Abelard left St. Mark's school two hours early and walked all the way to the tavern. The Golden Rose was busy. Dozens of patrons crowded the bar, discussing the various inquests. Abelard pushed his way through, up the back stairs and into the private apartments. Bingham was in his room. He was lying down on his bed, trying to sleep.

It was a grand room, like a model, like a room on display at a store. The walls were papered with castles. The bed featured quilts made from belly wool, from the finest of Swiss alpine goats. Toys were everywhere. On the two shelves under the windows. In the toy chest by the bed. In the cabinet that sagged from their weight in the corner. Of every description: toy soldiers and wagons and balls; model horses and Roman ballista; tops and puzzles and whistles and boats. I'd never been in Bingham's room before, and it amazed me. But Abelard simply pushed past me. He poked at his friend. He poked and he said, "Listen, Bingham. I don't care what you do, but I'm telling the truth."

Bingham rolled over onto one elbow. He yawned. "Oh, hi, Abelard. What did you say?"

"I don't know how you talked me into this mess, but I'm getting out . . . now. I'm telling the truth."

"What truth? Whose truth, Abelard? My truth or yours? And which will they believe? The truth about Dustin?"

"Look, I don't care about Dustin. I only care about me. And I . . . me." He skewered his chest with his finger. "I just can't take this anymore."

Bingham laughed. It was a light laugh. Oddly, he sounded like Arvin.

"Be still, Abelard. Try to calm yourself. You act as though you've just seen a ghost."

"I just did."

Bingham slapped him so hard that Abelard couldn't hear through one ear for three minutes. It just wouldn't stop ringing. Abelard crumbled. He slipped to his knees. He whimpered and whined like a dog. "This is the truth," Bingham said. "The pain that you feel on your face. This, and much worse, will become your existence, your sole reason for living, if you even consider betraying me. Banish it from your mind, Abelard."

He slapped him again, even harder. Abelard yelped, crawled away.

"Do you hear me?" said Bingham.

"I hear you." Abelard got to his feet. He rubbed his red face.

"That's better," said Bingham. He scratched at his chin. He pointed at the toy chest by his bed. "Now be a good lad and fetch me my bottle."

Ten minutes later, Abelard emerged from Bingham's room. The door closed behind him and Abelard stood for a moment, in the corridor, alone, simply rubbing his face. Well, alone save for me. He took his time descending the stairs. He wanted his face to cool down, for the blood to go back where it came from. The last thing he wanted was for someone to say, "Hey, what happened to you?" The well of his shame had no bottom. It ran as deep as the sea.

He was reminded of a potato-bag race he'd once run on Long Island, on some other excursion, before. He had lost his footing halfway down the course, and he'd started to tip, to career, then to crash into other contestants. He had fallen incredibly slowly, and landed with his face in the dirt.

That's how he felt now. He was careening from one disaster, from one nightmare, to the next. First the Lamp Room and the fire. Then the trial and his false statement. And now this thing with Dustin. It was all too much. Too much! It overwhelmed him. He actually liked Dustin. Sometimes he felt as if he simply couldn't breathe, as if his lungs were filling up with smoke. As if he were still *there*. *The truth. The truth*. He couldn't dislodge the words. They choked him, like two clumps of meat in his throat. *The truth*.

"Abelard? Abelard, is that you?"

"Yes, sir," he answered.

Otto Goldstein appeared at the head of the stairs. "I thought it was you. What's the matter? What happened? Your face."

"Nothing," he answered, trying to cover his cheek.

"Is Bingham receiving?"

"I'm just going, Herr Goldstein. Excuse me." He tried to slip by, but Goldstein was blocking the path. "Excuse me," he said with more vigor.

Goldstein snatched at the hand that was masking his face. "Abelard," he said. The boy's entire left cheekbone was livid. Goldstein took him by the hand. "Come with me for a moment, won't you, Abelard? If you don't mind. It's time we had a little chat."

CHAPTER 11

June 22, 1904
New York City

Unlike Henry Lundberg, Frank A. Barnaby wore a business suit. It was eminently plain. His posture was that of a soldier, although—save for two years in military academy as a boy—Barnaby had spent no time under any flag but his own. His great-grandfather had been born a rich man, as had his grandfather, his father, and he. The Knickerbocker Steamboat Company was only one of many ventures in which his family had interests. He was not a man to be trifled with, and O'Gorman found himself straightening, sitting up, as Barnaby mounted the dais.

The official recorder came forward. "Raise your right hand," he intoned. "Place your left hand on the Bible."

Barnaby dropped a hand on the book. O'Gorman was astounded. In all his years as coroner, after countless opportunities to scan and analyze and generally appraise the body parts of countless corpses, he had never seen a hand as beautiful as Frank A. Barnaby's. The long thin fingers were immaculate, the nails polished and shined. No dirt malingered under any nail.

"Do you solemnly swear . . ." And he did. Barnaby sat down. His movements were unhurried, casual, though planned; as if he were leaning back to read the newspaper in his favorite easy chair on Sunday morning after church. He and his attorneys had spent much time deliberating upon his demeanor.

"This panel would like to thank you, Mr. Barnaby, for taking the time to speak with us today," said O'Gorman. "We know how busy you are."

Barnaby lifted his arm with great weariness, tilted his wrist, and flipped his fingers over in a gesture of graceful dismissal. Then he sat there and stared at the crowd. He was but one man, confronted by so many, and yet each face he looked upon turned away. His gaze was like frost on a field. It chilled and congealed. He had the eyes of something dead.

O'Gorman started with a routine set of questions, confirming Barnaby's identity, his title and responsibilities. He asked about the firm's financial health, assets and debits. He inquired about the makeup of the board, who was responsible for what. His tone was modulated, clear, and unconfrontational. It was only when he asked about the life vests that I sensed his agitation.

"And how often, Mr. Barnaby, do you replenish the vessels?"

"That depends on what requires replenishment. Again, as I

said earlier, I don't concern myself with day-to-day details. Mine is an administrative post. You don't find me climbing about the rigging, as it were. My rigging is the annual report, my cables the columns in my ledgers. As chairman of the board, it is our shareholders who concern me. The value of our stock."

"Let's talk about the life vests."

"What about them?"

"How often are they replenished, replaced, rotated out? How often do you change them?"

Barnaby raised his eyebrow. A young clerk jumped to attention. He took a step forward, leaned down, and whispered into the hairy ear of Cornelius Plimpton, of Thompson, Peabody, Wilson and Plimpton, attorneys-at-law: New York–Philadelphia. Plimpton pulled at his nose and Barnaby visibly softened.

"I'm afraid I don't know. Again, that's something that you'll have to ask Van Schaick, or someone in inventory control."

O'Gorman rolled up his lips. "Well, Mr. Barnaby, let's try it from a different angle, shall we? Do you or do you not recall ever getting any requests from Captain Van Schaick for new life vests?"

"Once again, please understand that such requests don't go to me personally, as a rule, but to someone in inventory control. We have a central clearinghouse for disbursement. Everything from new scuppers, to anchor chains, to life jackets. Everything comes out of our Brooklyn yard. O'Malley's the bursar. I think that's his name. He could tell you. Perhaps you know him."

O'Gorman took a deep breath. "I'm afraid I haven't had the

pleasure of meeting that particular Irish American. Now, Mr. Barnaby. Are you telling me that you have no record, not even in accounting, of requests from Van Schaick for new life vests?"

"Life jackets. I didn't say that. I'm sure that if such a request—"

"Requests. Plural, Mr. Barnaby. Allegedly, three separate requests. Over a period of seventeen months."

"If such requests were addressed, there would indeed be a notation in the ledgers. We track the cost of maintenance for every ship. They each have their own P and L. But all this is moot. You're wasting your time, sir, and mine. I have on my person, at this moment, definitive proof that new life jackets were on order for the *General Slocum*." Barnaby slipped his right hand in his coat. He removed a piece of paper, displayed it to the audience, like a magic trick, and then returned it at once to his jacket.

"Mr. Barnaby, the fact that live vests may or may not have been on order wasn't particularly helpful to the men, women, and children who burned to death on your steamboat. Eyewitness after eyewitness has testified that the life vests either crumbled in their hands or soaked up so much water that they dragged whoever wore them down. The very thing that was meant to save them," said O'Gorman, "the instrument of their salvation, turned out to be responsible for their deaths. Ironic, don't you think?"

"Irony, Coroner, is a thing best left to playwrights and professors. I deal in facts, sir. In dollars and sense. I manage a business that employs hundreds of people, that feeds a good many more than a thousand. Do not be maudlin, sir. I, too, have feelings. I have a wife, and a mother and sister, and nieces and nephews and cousins. Let us stick to the facts, sir. I elect not to march in your sentiment parade."

"There was nothing sentimental about dragging dead babies out of the surf for a week," said O'Gorman. "Especially after the crabs had been at 'em."

A collective gasp filled the room. O'Gorman looked up at the balcony, at my sister Louisa. Through me.

"I'm not interested in sentiment," he continued. "I'm only interested in justice, Mr. Barnaby. Which can only come from the truth. I don't particularly care what the USSIS reported, or failed to report. You're an independent business making independent profits. It's unseemly to cry on the federal shoulder at this date. For years you've been filling your coffers with pennies from the pockets of immigrants. From church groups like the one at St. Mark's."

"Profits are fuel to the engine of industry, not merely a by-product," said Barnaby. "Profits enable capital improvement. Without them, there would be no life jackets, new or old. And profits drive shareholder value, rewarding the ultimate stakeholders. Who are these villains? Are they the gluttonous demons portrayed in socialist rags? No, sir. They are not. They're generally pension funds, the collective investments of thousands and thousands of ordinary people—schoolteachers and merchants, businessmen, clerks, policemen, construction workers, cashiers; your mother and father, and"—he paused for effect—"most probably *you*."

"A rousing and most excellent lesson," said O'Gorman. "But

we're not here to debate economics, or to indict the capitalist system. I just want to know one more thing."

"What is that, sir?"

"How far does it go?"

"Does what go?"

"How high, how deep, and how far?"

"Be clear, man. How far does what go?"

"The responsibility," said O'Gorman. "When a company encourages imbibing with inspectors. When it fails to heed warnings from its own employees. For seventeen months, mind you. Issued on three occasions. How high, how deep, how far does it go?"

"I refuse to answer that question on the grounds that it may incriminate me. I know my rights, O'Gorman. The Fifth Amendment clearly states: 'nor shall [he] be compelled in any criminal case to be a witness against himself.'"

"How far?"

"I object, sir!" Cornelius Plimpton staggered to his feet. He was a willowy old man, graceful and tall, with the bearing and affectations of a Southern gentleman. He wore a light cotton suit with blue stripes. He carried a mahogany cane with a lion-head handle, and his longish white hair fell in traces about his thin face, lending his noble appearance a certain unpredictable quality, a wildness.

"The witness has already invoked his rights under the Fifth Amendment. Kindly move on, sir. Try a new line of questioning."

O'Gorman looked down upon Plimpton. To the coroner, the

attorney's face was hawklike and predatory. If he were a Southern gentleman, he was lounging about his tobacco plantation, on some majestic veranda, waiting to mete out a beating. "I want to establish if Mr. Barnaby and the rest of his board feel any responsibility for what happened. Do they feel themselves culpable?"

"The statutes," said Plimpton, "are clear. You may link Van Schaick to the corporation, but the corporation itself . . . Well, it can hardly be accused of manslaughter."

"Why is that? I think Barnaby and the entire board are liable under the Act of 1871—CH 100, 56, 16. Statute 456."

Plimpton laughed. He placed a hand on his hip; he turned and smiled at the crowd. "The corporation cannot be convicted of the substantive offense. It cannot 'suffer the punishment of confinement at hard labor for a period of not more than ten years.' It's a corporation; not a person."

"You're arguing that the corporation can't be liable—and, therefore, the officers of the board—simply because the corporate entity can't go to jail?"

"The statutes are clear."

"This is an inquest, not a trial. Let the courts try and figure out that one. But I believe a corporation can—and, in this case, *should* be indicted for manslaughter. You, your board, and your company failed to provide, in violation of federal law, either proper lifesaving or firefighting equipment. And while the current statute may not prescribe punishment, it blessedly absolves me of proving intent. No," said O'Gorman, shaking his head. "I fear you hold your passengers in such contempt, such thoughtless derision, that intent would imply far too sullying an effort on your part. There was no killing by intent. It was murder by neglect, perhaps, or by incompetence. At worst, due to unthinking greed."

"I object," Plimpton cried. "This panel has no jurisdiction on this issue. This is harassment, Coroner. And highly prejudicial."

"*You* object! Thankfully, counsel, I'm a coroner, not a judge. I spend my day surrounded by dead people. By the time they get to me, all the damage they're ever going to do has already been done. *You* object!" He laughed grimly, shook his head. "*I* object, counsel. *I* object to your client's fractured memory, his facile evidence, and his well-rehearsed and condescending tone. I object to any man who does something wrong and then doesn't face up to it, who can't take his medicine." He stood up. He leaned to the side. Then he pointed at Barnaby. "I object to you, sir," he said. "And to all of your board."

"I will not be made your sacrificial lamb," said Barnaby. His voice was cool, serene. "To say that I, in my office, am linked to this incident, belies the league upon league of anchor chain between us. Fault me for failing to pump up our stock, for eroding shareholder value, and I'll gladly step down from my post—take my lumps. But will you make me culpable for Van Schaick's decision to keep sailing north, for the cowardice of seamen I've never met, for the inattentiveness of officers directly responsible for ensuring their ship stays in tip-top condition? Indeed, will you hold me responsible for another man's cigarette?"

O'Gorman smiled unctuously. "I'd like you to do me a favor," he said.

"A favor?"

"Yes, sir. If you would."

"This is highly improper . . ." Plimpton started.

O'Gorman held up his hand, and Plimpton sat back in his seat. A pall settled over the chambers.

For the first time during the inquest, Barnaby looked uncomfortable. He shifted almost imperceptibly. He coughed and said, "That depends."

O'Gorman smiled. "Picture your ledgers, Mr. Barnaby. You can do it. Close your eyes. Look *real* close. You see that comma? In the fifth volume; on the fourth page; in the third column. Mixed in with all those numbers. All those digits. All of that wealth. Can you see it? I know it's difficult. It's so damned small and insignificant. Why, that's no comma at all, although it looks like one. That's no speck of ink, Mr. Barnaby. That's nothing but a mother's tear."

It was a cloudy night. A front had swept in from the west, and raindrops spattered the skylight. It was humid and hot. Lightning clawed at the sky. It felt like it would never stop raining.

Dustin was sleeping alone; Henrik was working a double, and Mrs. Silverstein snored on the sofa next door. I came in through the skylight this time. I reasoned that if I came in from above, the room might stay warm a bit longer. But it didn't work. As soon as I descended, I saw the breath around his mouth start to whiten.

Dustin curled inward. He nuzzled his blanket and turned. I saw his face then, lit up by lightning. It glimmered and shone. Lines of rain on the skylight cast shadows that mottled his cheekbones and brow. Like tears. Shadow tears.

I knelt down beside him. His eyes rolled relentlessly under his lids. He was dreaming, but I couldn't see it. He was somewhere at sea once again. I resisted the urge to climb back in his head. I wanted to be where I was, at his side. I leaned forward. I admired his delicate eyebrows. I admired his nose, and his cheekbones, and lips. I reached down, I leaned over and kissed him. There. It's done. He flinched, reflexively. At the cold. I watched ice crystals form on his lips and then melt. He opened his mouth. I watched as a droplet fell in.

His eyes opened, and he stared at me, right in my face. Right there! He was terrified, I could feel it, but he would not withdraw. He didn't recoil or retreat. He stood fast. And he reached with his hand, trying to touch me, although there was nothing to see. He reached out and I felt him, his fingers, on my cheek. I could feel him.

Find her. Miss Hall. Touch her hand. Even to me, the words seemed unearthly and alien. I didn't know where they had come from.

Dustin pulled back. He clutched at the blanket. He tried to sit up but his legs were not working.

Touch her hand, I repeated, and she knocked.

Even in the servants' quarters, the banging was clear. Dustin leaped to his feet. He ran to the sitting room. Mrs. Silverstein was lighting a candle. He opened the door. The knocking was coming from someplace below. He ran down the steps. Someone stirred in the captain's apartments. He could hear people milling about. The pounding continued. He made it downstairs. Dustin opened the door, I slipped out and passed through her.

"Mallory!"

"No, it's me," said Louisa. She collapsed in his arms. She was soaking with rain.

Dustin jumped. For a moment, he thought. For the briefest of instants . . . But as old lady Silverstein descended the stairs, he could see who reclined in his arms. My sister Louisa. Not me.

"What's the matter?" said Dustin. "What are you doing here?"

"Your father," she said, out of breath. "Your father—they're holding him. They say if you don't come, they'll deliver him to the police." Louisa pressed herself close. "They say that he's guilty of murder, an accomplice. I'm sorry. I'm so sorry, Dustin; I know it's not true. I had to come find you. I just had to. I'm sorry."

"What for?" he replied. He stroked her wet hair. He pushed it away from her face. She was crying. "Stop that, do you hear me? Everything's going to be all right. I know what I have to do."

"You're going to give yourself up?"

"If I have to, but that's not what I meant. No, something else."

"What?"

"I have to see Miss Hall. Of the Knickerbocker Steamboat Company. I have to see her, tonight."

"Why? What are you talking about?"

"I can't explain. It's just something I have to do. Like a promise."

"A promise? A promise to whom?"

Dustin looked up at the sky. The rain was finally tapering off. For a moment, the moon became visible, a bright flash between clouds, just a sliver. And then it was gone. He looked down at Louisa's face. How strange, he thought, that he had never really seen her face before. This wasn't Mallory's sister. Or one of the Meer girls. This face belonged to somebody else. "It's hard to explain," he said.

"A promise to Mallory?"

Dustin nodded.

"You've felt her?"

"Have you?"

She nodded and sighed. "Every night." She looked back at Dustin. "She told me to find you. She said you'd be here."

Dustin smiled. "I want you to go to my father. Go to my father, Louisa, and tell him I'm coming. Tell him not to give up."

"What about you?"

"I'll be there soon. Tell my father."

Louisa descended the steps. Then she stopped. She turned swiftly and said, "It's because of your promise. Your promise to Mallory, isn't it?"

"Yes."

"Do you still love her, Dustin?"

He smiled a little smile. He stood there and stared as I waited. As I waited and empires fell, and continents faded to nothing. I waited. "I'll always love her," he said. "Just as you do, Louisa. But she's dead now."

"If she's dead, why doesn't she just go away?"

CHAPTER 12

June 22, 1904
New York City

Bingham lay on his bedroom floor, peering through a knothole at the revelers below. It was a rowdy crowd tonight. Ingrid, one of the prettier barmaids, was having a hard time fending off the advances of Hans Gutterman, a strapping young cooper from Düsseldorf. Each time that she slipped by his table, he'd reach out and pull at her dress. He fondled her hips. He squeezed her and called her his *Säugamme*, his wet nurse.

Bingham liked Ingrid. He strained to get a better look at her cleavage when another face popped into view. At this hour of the night! His friend Lehman was up late.

Bingham rolled to his knees. He popped the knot of wood into place. Once covered, his spy hole was practically invisible. He stepped on the plug for good measure. Then he flopped on his bed, picked up a book, flipped through some pages, and waited. Moments later, Karl Lehman knocked on the door.

"Come in, Karl," he answered.

"How did you know?"

Bingham put down the book on his chest. "I always know when it's you, Karl. You have a very distinctive knock."

"I do?"

"Everyone does. If you know how to listen."

Long ago, Bingham had discovered that he was most comfortable when surrounded by the discomfort of others. He seethed when others were settled. He worried and sulked when they laughed. But when they were troubled, nervous or frightened, when they quaked with anxiety, panic, a strange peace overcame him. He found balance in chaos. He found solace. It was this characteristic, as sure as the lumps on his head, that marked him for greatness. In battle, most likely, he thought, where less favored men usually faltered.

"What are you leering at, Lehman?" said Bingham. His friend was suddenly beaming. "Why are you even here?"

"It's Dustin," he said. "He's been spotted. He was seen in Kleindeutschland this evening."

Bingham leaped to his feet. At last, here was his chance. Here was his moment to shine. And not merely in front of his father— before everyone. "Where?"

"On Fourteenth Street and Sixth, heading south."

"When?"

"Twenty minutes ago."

Bingham smacked his lips. He patted his friend on the back. "Well done, Karl," he said. He was jubilant. He lunged for his jacket. Then he paused. "Wait a minute," he added. He knelt by his toy chest. He opened the top. There! By his drum and his jack-in-the-box. By the bronze busts of Wilhelm I and the Empress Augusta, his wife. He rummaged about. By the sock with his bottle of schnapps lay his belt, and his scabbard, and knife.

"What do you need that for?"

Bingham grinned. He stuffed the knife in his belt. "Just in case."

By the time Dustin got to the offices of the Knickerbocker Steamboat Company, the rain had stopped falling. Clouds scudded across the sky. But the storm had died down. The lightning had ceased. And the wind had tired of blowing.

Dustin waited and waited and waited, in an alleyway just down the street. He knew that, at some point, she'd go by him. He'd already made sure; he'd inquired within. And besides, he could sense it. Miss Hall was still working upstairs.

Dustin lit a cigarette. He tossed the match to the ground, looked up—across the carriages and cars that streamed along the street, across the crowded sidewalk—and counted off the windows on the seventh floor. Three, four, five, and there she was. The window still shimmered with rain.

He couldn't see Miss Hall as she sat there, as she tidied her figures, bent over—like a seamstress, like a diamond cutter—transcribing columns of numbers, but I could. And he couldn't see me as I floated, disembodied, in the sky above Broadway, just a flash on a backdrop of lightning. Clouds gathered like bulls in the night, butting horns. The wind gathered speed. The air was still heavy with rain.

Miss Hall stood, stretched and yawned all at once. She slipped off her work shoes—dark navy blue flats. She wiggled them into a bag. Then she slipped on her booties and jacket, the one with the piping and overcast stitches, and turned off the light on her desk. It was eleven o'clock. Well past teatime or supper. Well past bedtime. She made for the window, cracked it open, sniffed the air, and gaped at the traffic below.

Who were all these people? she wondered. Where were they going, and what for? She shook her head. She closed the window, shuddered, and looked back at her desk. The world was a fickle companion, a mislabeled plan, a lifetime spent pining for some married man. But here, in the world of her ledgers, she thought, numbers lined up in parallel columns, in predictable rows. Numbers tallied and matched; they subtracted politely, added up without pride, multiplied without hubris, and divided with grace. They never, ever lied to you first. They were as honest as you were.

Miss Hall picked up her umbrella. She shook it once, to be sure, and then made for the door. I watched her as she shuffled downstairs. I watched her as she crossed the foyer, spun through the brass revolving door, and stepped outside where Dustin waited.

She looked up at the sky. It had stopped raining. For a moment, she agonized over whether or not to open her umbrella. Then she thought, *Take a chance! Take a risk, just for once.* And she smiled to herself as she furled the umbrella, snapped the band.

Dustin stepped out. His pace was deliberate, slow, compared with the others who darted about on the sidewalk. It was quite dark now. Clouds massed overhead. It looked like it was going to rain, once again. But Dustin didn't care. He was gathering his thoughts. He was focused, directed. He was thinking of me.

Miss Hall progressed down the street, then looked up and saw Dustin, and paused for the briefest of moments. She continued, undaunted. She passed right beside him, he turned, said her name. Just like that. "Miss Hall." Not even a question; a relaying of facts. "Miss Hall," Dustin said, and she turned. She stopped as he reached for her fingers. Her hand, she pulled back, but he swept in beside her. He touched her; she looked at his face. In that instant, Dustin saw everything—each terrible memory, each scene as it passed through the bridge of his fingers.

Miss Hall turned and retreated. Dustin staggered away. He lifted his face to the night sky and screamed. Then Bingham hit him.

It happened so quickly that I wasn't prepared. I'd missed them all circling about. Bingham and Lehman and a few other friends, in a pack, in a phalanx around him. Dustin wheeled. Blood poured from his face. Bingham's punch had split both of his lips. It was terribly red on his teeth. It was livid. Dustin spat, shook his head. Then he charged.

He struck with such force, such velocity, that Bingham spun about like a puppet and fell. Dustin was on him in seconds. He punched at his face. Twice, three times. Bingham screamed like a girl. He kept screaming until Lehman pulled Dustin away. Then they held him. They all did. And Bingham got up. He approached with that knife in his hand. His face looked horrific; his nose had been broken. Blood dripped on his summer-weight coat. "Now it's your turn," he said. The blade danced in his hand. "For Klein-deutschland."

He thrust, but the knife struck at me. It grew terribly cold. Bingham screeched. He opened his fingers, turned his hand. The blade was stuck fast to his palm. He shook it, he screamed, but it wouldn't come free. He dropped to his knees. "Get it off me!" he pleaded. "Get it off."

The knife slipped to the street. Bingham rolled like a ball on his side.

Dustin pulled free. The boys stood about. They were speechless. They looked down at young Goldstein, at his arm. It was frozen and blue. It was covered in ice. Dustin picked up the knife.

The boys stepped to the side. They retreated.

"Don't worry," said Dustin. "I'm not going to hurt you." He tossed the knife down the street. "Get up, Bingham," he added. He stretched out his hand. He dragged the boy to his feet. Then he stared at the sky. "Looks like rain again," he said. "And we've got an appointment to keep."

CHAPTER 13

June 22, 1904
New York City

As soon as **Miss Hall had been touched** on the street, she began to see everything clearly. The memories struck her in waves. First the smell of the smoke, then that scream; the first of so many. And the flames sweeping out of the officers' quarters. She remembered it just as I saw it. She was in me. I was in her. We were in there together.

Miss Hall ran. She went back to her office; it was closer than home. And in some ways it was safer. She belonged there. It was the place where she suffered most plainly. *Life jackets were already on order.*

The memories deluged her as she ascended the stairs, made her way down the hall, as she pressed her thin back to the wall. She closed her eyes; it was easier. The visions washed through her like a tropical fever, a fit. *You can change a number in a column*, she thought. *But once you do, it's never the same. One number altered alters others, until the whole thing comes undone. One dropped stitch and it's ruined.*

And we were standing on the hurricane deck once again. Children were burning in torrents of flame, in rivers of fire. They drowned. Their skin popped and sizzled. It bubbled and peeled. We could smell it. Or was that just the hair in our noses? We could feel it as the fire drew near. "Mallory," someone said. It was Dustin behind me. He was holding a life vest. He had managed to save one for me.

Miss Hall leaned against the office door. She fumbled with the lock and burst through. Her desk was framed by a shadow. She rushed into the room. She lunged for her chair. Her chair! Her ledgers! With her nails, she clawed at her desk.

Just for me, yes, you told me. So I wore it. And it fit perfectly. The fire approached down the deck. It was almost upon us. I turned and you pushed me. I fell. When you pushed me, I fell. And I drowned.

Miss Hall slumped on her desk. She was panting. Her mouth—it was dry. It was dry as a bone. And worse, it still tasted of smoke.

PART III

CHAPTER 14

June 23, 1904
New York City

Miss Hall sat on the dais without speaking. She looked down at her shoes. Like her, they were showing their age.

"Would you like me to repeat the question?" said O'Gorman. "Miss Hall? Miss Hall!"

"No, Coroner, that won't be necessary." Miss Hall plucked a kerchief from out of her sleeve. She pressed it to her face. She wanted to eat it. She wanted to stuff it down her own throat. "About the life preservers," she said.

"That's right. Here, let me refresh your memory." He leaned forward. He handed a ledger to the official recorder, who carried it over to the witness.

Miss Hall opened the book. She examined the pages with care. "Yes, these are the figures for the *General Slocum*."

"Is there a line there for life vests, Miss Hall?"

"I suppose so."

"You suppose! Aren't these numbers your handiwork? Look at the page that I earmarked. Look at it closely. You see line fourteen?"

"Yes, I see it."

"What does it say in the legend?"

"It says 'life preservers.'"

"Life vests, life preservers, life jackets. What's the difference?"

"Life preservers do just that. They preserve life."

Upstairs, the gallery simmered.

"Not if they crumble in your hands," said O'Gorman.

Miss Hall turned away. She pressed the kerchief to her face.

"So, there is a line for life preservers, after all. Isn't that right? Isn't that right, my dear?" said O'Gorman.

"My name is Miss Hall."

"Come now, Miss Hall. Don't be churlish."

"Churlish?" Miss Hall laughed. It was high-pitched and nervous. Then she stopped, without warning. She looked at the crowd. "Ask your questions," she said. Her smile was sublime. It was barely a wrinkle. She stared at O'Gorman and said, "Ask away."

"This number on the side."

"The date."

"Yes, the date. In your sworn affidavit you state, and I read, 'Life jackets were already on order.'"

"Life preservers."

O'Gorman looked over the table. "I'm quoting your testimony, Miss Hall, nothing more. I call them life vests. You call them life preservers. And life jackets . . ." O'Gorman's hands danced about on his desk. He rifled through papers. "Who calls them life jackets? I forget now, remind me," he said to the official recorder. "No, wait. I remember. Don't tell me." He paused. "Frank A. Barnaby." He raised his right eyebrow. "The president of the Knickerbocker Steamboat Company. The man you report to, whose desk sits nearby, whose needs you've attended for years." He smiled stiffly. "The date, Miss Hall."

"I take umbrage at your gross insinuation."

"The date."

"What about it?"

"It's been changed, it appears. Can't you see? It was one date and now it's another."

Miss Hall stared at her shoes. She tucked her chin to her chest. She glanced at the crowd and said, "People assume I'm a spinster. I don't blame them, of course. It's quite natural. I mean, look at me." She poked at her hair. Then she smiled. "But it's not really true; I was married once. It was a long time ago."

A hush purged the chambers.

"I'm not fashionable. I try to dress well, but my salary is small. And my husband . . . I make do. I scrimp and I save. Naturally," she continued, "people assume that I'm vulnerable, weak. After all, I'm a woman. They assume such things because I'm frail to look at. Because I've been at the same job, doing the same work, for almost twenty years." She looked up at the audience and smiled. "But appearances can be deceiving. When one assumes about me, one does so at one's peril." She stared at Cornelius Plimpton. "The date looks like it's been altered because it was."

"Excuse me," said O'Gorman. "What did you say?"

"The date. I changed it. No life preservers were on order. No life vests or life jackets. The date was the launch of the vessel."

"You changed it. Why? At whose urging?"

"Mr. Barnaby's."

The crowd roared, and Cornelius Plimpton leaped to his feet. "I object to this testimony. This is highly irregular. Why, it's simply her word against his."

O'Gorman stood up and the audience grew still. "If you please, sir," he shouted. Then he turned. "I'm so sorry, Miss Hall. Did I hear you correctly?" he said. "Mr. Barnaby, Frank A. Barnaby, the president of the Knickerbocker Steamboat Company, told you to alter the records?"

"Yes, he did."

"But your previous testimony, your own affidavit . . ."

"I lied."

O'Gorman sat down. The crowd murmured and seethed.

"Well, if she lied then . . ." added Plimpton.

"Be quiet, or I'll have you removed," said O'Gorman.

Cornelius Plimpton retreated.

"Yes, Miss Hall," said O'Gorman. "Mr. Plimpton does have a point. How can we be sure that you're telling the truth now? Why the sudden change of heart?"

Miss Hall only shrugged. She stared at her shoes. "I didn't know then," she answered. Then she looked at the crowd. She smiled and said, "I have my reasons."

An object hit Plimpton square on the head. He turned and cursed under his breath. Then another, and another. They poured down from above. Small and silver and shiny and wiggling. Silversides—tiny fish used as bait. They were fresh from the sea. Almost transparent, with bright shiny scales. I could see their hearts pumping inside them.

"Order," said O'Gorman, though without much conviction. "I said order," he added halfheartedly.

Plimpton raised a fat book to his head. Fish kept showering down from above. They splattered and stuck; they wiggled and fell. "Murderer," someone shouted. "Murderer." Plimpton dashed from the chambers in a rainstorm of grunion. He was gone at a run and the crowd lost momentum. The pelting subsided. There was no one to pelt. He was gone, after all, and his client Frank Barnaby hadn't bothered to come.

Chapter 15

June 23, 1904
New York City

Dustin appeared at the back of the hall. A hush fell on the room like a dusting of snow. No one moved. No one fidgeted. They barely breathed as he mounted the dais.

He looked terrible. He was dressed in the same clothes he'd been wearing for weeks—a tattered pair of wool pants, a white shirt and black jacket. He hadn't shaved. He hadn't slept. He hadn't eaten. He'd spent the whole evening locked in the cellar with Arvin. They had talked all night long. They had talked about everything: the old country—about castles and farms, the marshes of Schlüsselburg; about brewing; and God. They'd even talked of his mother, Tabea. Arvin had stared at the brew vats and wept.

Dustin sat on the chair. He brushed at his hair. His eyes looked puffy from crying. He stared at Abelard, Bingham, and Karl. They were sitting in front, on a long wooden bench. They were dressed in immaculate suits. And Goldstein presided, surrounded by Munch, Max, and Bering.

It was a frightening frieze, with my love pressed between them, like a flower within two panes of glass. The room smelled of grunion. Most of the spectators had come from the coroner's inquest, and their hands were still covered in scales.

"Please stand," Goldstein said.

Dustin struggled to his feet. He was exhausted.

Goldstein motioned and a small man stepped up to the dais. He was carrying a Bible.

"Or, if you prefer," Goldstein said, "we can look for a Torah."

"That won't be necessary." Dustin gave up a smile. "I'm a Marxist," he said. "God is dead."

A murmur ripped through the audience. Louisa looked down from the balcony. Her heart swelled with sorrow.

"Perhaps to you, sir," Goldstein said. "But to me, and to the people of Kleindeutschland, He still reigns supreme. Will you give me your word, then? Do you swear to tell the truth, the whole truth, and nothing but the truth . . ."

"Free my father, and I'll tell you whatever you want."

"Just the truth, please," said Goldstein.

Dustin turned and looked up. His eyes were shiny and bright. "The truth, as I see it?" he said. "Are you sure? Even if it's uncolored by some temperamental deity with Lutheran misgivings? Untainted by capitalist obsession? Unsullied by a hunger for revenge, an overriding drive to get the bastards who killed your sister or your mother or your . . ." He took a breath. "I'll tell you what I can remember. Nothing more."

"Very well, then," said Goldstein. "Sit down."

Dustin dropped to the chair, closed his eyes, and took several deep breaths. After a moment, he said, "You know, it's funny, but while I'll never ever forget that afternoon, it's the things that happened that morning, before the fire, which I remember most clearly. Little things. Glimpses. Like those couples dancing their waltzes. And dresses ballooning. The parasols—all those colors in motion. The laughter . . . Our last moments of innocence, when everything was still normal. Like it used to be. But I guess you only want to hear about the fire."

"Tell us about the Lamp Room, Dustin. If you would. Tell us exactly what happened."

Dustin smiled. "Very well," he said. "It was as your son and Karl and Abelard reported. Well, almost." He looked down at the bench in front. "Mallory and I were in the Lamp Room, just forward of the coal bin and boiler."

"Why were you there?"

"Why?" He looked up at the balcony, as if he could sense my presence near the ceiling. "Because I was in love with her."

The dining hall echoed with whispers. Goldstein raised his hand. "With Mallory Meer?"

Dustin nodded. I felt myself glow. Now everyone in the whole neighborhood knew. Dustin Brauer is in love with me. With me! Or, at least, he was.

"Go on."

"It had been too busy on the main deck. Men from the galley kept circling about. So we descended a level, and the Lamp Room was there, up ahead. It was empty." He paused. "Before Bingham joined us. Anyway, he made some comment about my being at a St. Mark's function. He called us some names. Then he and Abelard and Karl went aloft. Mallory soon joined them. And, after a few minutes, I did, too."

"Not so fast there, young Brauer. Let's not gloss over the truth."

"Ah yes, the truth," said Dustin. "The truth is I stayed behind to collect my thoughts and have a cigarette. The truth is I'd never kissed a girl before, not until then. That's what I wanted to think about. Not your son."

"What about the cigarette?"

"I put it out. I dropped it to the floor, I stamped it out with my heel—as I always do. Then I left."

"Are you absolutely sure? Isn't it possible that, after your alter-cation, after your first kiss, as you said, it might have just slipped from your mind?"

"I suppose," Dustin answered.

"You suppose?"

"What do you want me to say? That I'm guilty? That I started that fire? What does it matter?" He looked up at Louisa. His face was twisted with pain. "I *am* guilty."

"What did you say?" Goldstein leaned forward.

"You heard me. I said I'm guilty." He shook his head. "I was standing there with that thing in my hand. I had wrestled it away from some cowardly man. And I came to her. I held it out. Like a gift."

"Held what out? What are you talking about?"

Dustin swam on the memory. "The life vest. I'd found one. So I made her put it on. There was no time to lose. The fire was practically on us. But she was frightened of jumping, I think. The water looked a long way away from the hurricane deck. So I pushed her. And she fell. Mallory. She vanished into the river. I looked down at the spot. I marked it. I watched, but she never came up. Not once." He stared up at Louisa. "I put her into that thing, and she sank like a stone. I drowned her."

"Ula," said Goldstein.

"Excuse me?"

Goldstein shook his head. "My wife," he replied. "She died on that steamship." He focused on Dustin. "I daresay there isn't a man in this dining hall who hasn't lost someone he loved."

Dustin looked spent. His eyelashes glimmered with tears. He started to speak, but the words didn't come.

"Abelard," Goldstein said. His face betrayed no emotion. "Abelard, take the chair, please."

"Is that it?" Dustin said. "Are you finished?"

"For now."

Abelard Warner got up from the bench. Bingham and Karl looked surprised. Dustin stood up to make room for him.

"What is this?" Hans Bering cut in. "We've already heard from this boy."

"He has more to tell us," said Goldstein.

"About what? Now see here," said Max. "Brauer's admitted his guilt."

"We're all guilty."

"Excuse me?"

Goldstein stared out at the audience. Then he looked down at his son. "Is there something you want to say, Bingham?"

"No, Father."

Goldstein sighed. He motioned toward Abelard. The boy took the witness chair.

"Remember. You're still under oath," Goldstein said.

The boy nodded. His head sagged on his chest.

"Tell us what happened," said Goldstein. "Once again, if you please. You went down to the Lamp Room . . ."

"Me and Bingham and Karl. We went down to the Lamp Room, belowdecks. Bingham was looking for Mallory. He said that he wanted to see her."

"Why's that?"

"Bingham has . . . had a thing for her. He liked her, I guess. He wouldn't leave her alone. He went on and on about the blouse she was wearing."

"I see. And then what?"

"Then we saw them together. They were kissing, and Bingham went crazy."

"What do you mean, he went crazy? How? What did he do?"

"He told Dustin he shouldn't be there, on a Lutheran outing, being a Jew. He called him Bauer instead of Brauer, like he always does, and he called Mallory 'tainted meat.'"

"He called her that?"

Abelard nodded. "Then we left. Moments later, so did Mallory. We hovered off to the side, near the coal bin. We could hear her climbing the stairs. Dustin stayed behind. That's when he lit that cigarette. We could see it. We could see him smoking there in the dark."

"And then?"

"Then he tossed it to the deck."

"Did it roll?"

Abelard looked down at the bench. He looked at the feet of his friends, but he was loath to look higher.

"Did it roll, Abelard?"

"No, it didn't. He stamped it right out with his heel. As he said."

The dining hall burst into chatter. Somebody whistled. Goldstein lifted his hand. "Then what?" he continued. "What happened next?"

"Dustin left the Lamp Room. A few minutes later, Bingham and Karl and I followed him down the hall toward the stairs. But

Bingham pulled off. He went back to the Lamp Room. So we followed. He was angry. You know how he gets. He was in one of his cold moods again."

"Father!" cried Bingham. He leaped to his feet.

"Be still, child. You had your chance to speak earlier." He turned back to Abelard. "Continue," he said.

Abelard hesitated.

"Go on, boy. Continue. What happened next?"

"Bingham lit up a cigarette and smoked it without speaking. Karl and I wanted to go back upstairs, but we were scared to disturb him. Then he finished his cigarette and flicked it. But he flicked it too hard, and it went sailing into this box full of straw. He ran over to it—to snatch the butt out, I guess—but it started to burn. Then he laughed. He looked down at the fire and said, 'Let the Jew take the blame, he deserves it.' We thought it would be easy to douse, to control. We thought someone, a crewman, would quench it . . . and blame Dustin. How could we have know what would happen?"

The crowd roared.

"Indeed," Goldstein said. "How could we?" He nodded and said, "That will be quite enough, thank you, Abelard." He twisted toward Max to his left. "Don't you think?" He looked at both Bering and Munch on his right.

"Of course," Max replied. "As you wish, Otto."

"I'm sorry," said Bering.

Goldstein smiled tightly. He stood, then stepped back. He

looked down at his son on the bench. Bingham sat there, still perfectly still. Goldstein moved from the dais and approached him. "This inquest is over. The meeting's adjourned."

"What about Bingham?" somebody shouted. "It was his cigarette," another man said. "He's the one started the fire."

Goldstein stepped up to the bench. He looked out at the people. They were milling about. They were jockeying for an optimal view. "This inquest is over, do you hear me? I lost a wife less than two weeks ago. I don't plan on losing a son. If there is any man here," he said, "anyone who thinks otherwise, let him step up to me now."

No one spoke. No one said anything.

"Now get the hell out of my bar."

CHAPTER 16

June 23, 1904
New York City

Dustin and Goldstein went down the back stairs. My father and Louisa soon followed. Arvin was imprisoned behind the last door, at the end of a very long corridor. Goldstein pulled out his key chain. He selected a key. He unlocked the lock and stepped forward.

Dustin's father was sitting near the rear of the cellar, his back to a beer barrel, trying to sleep. As soon as Arvin heard the door start to creak, he rolled to his feet. Goldstein hesitated. Dustin bounded within. He ran to his father. They collided, embraced. Arvin kissed Dustin right on the face.

"What happened?" said Arvin, finally catching his breath. "Are you here to free or to join me? Which is it?" And then, as

Goldstein drew near: "Which is it, Herr Goldstein? What do you plan to do with my son?"

"Set him free."

"So I can take you home," Dustin said. "Wherever that is." He explained to his father what had happened.

Goldstein touched Arvin on the shoulder. "Arvin," he said. "I know we've had our differences. I know we haven't always seen eye to eye. But I also know that Ula would have wanted you to stay. To continue to work here, at the Rose. Are you sure you won't reconsider? It just won't be the same here without you."

"Perhaps it will be better," Arvin said. "Mine is an itinerant class, after all. I've already stayed way too long. If it hadn't been for Ula . . ."

"Yes," Goldstein said. "If it hadn't been for Ula." Then he smiled and stepped back. "But where will you go? And for whom will you work?"

Arvin took Dustin by the hand. "We are used to the highway, aren't we, Dustin? We've traveled before. Perhaps to Minn-e-so-ta. I hear they are looking for men. Don't worry, Otto. I'll leave you a bowl of my yeast."

"Or Missouri," said Dustin. "And we're changing our name."

"To what?" Goldstein asked him.

"Who knows?" Arvin said. "It will come to us. Arvin Brauer belongs to the people now. It's no longer my name." He paused. "I bequeath it to them." Then he turned to face Goldstein. "Thank you for talking with Abelard. You did, didn't you? You spoke with him about telling the truth. It must have been terribly difficult, knowing that he'd implicate Bingham. Your own son."

"I've been accused of many things, Herr Brauer, as you know. But no one calls me a liar. A deal is a deal. That's simply good business."

"Ah yes, good business," Arvin said with a nod.

"It wasn't Bingham who started that fire." My father stepped forward. "It was bigotry, Arvin," he said. "Pure and simple. It was the hate in his heart."

Goldstein laughed mirthlessly. "A son's failings are a father's greatest failure. Besides, didn't you hear? Barnaby and Van Schaick. Even Lundberg, the inspector. They were all found guilty this morning." He replaced the cellar key on his chain. He put it back in his pocket. Then he started up the stairs once again. "My son," he added, over his shoulder. "My son was never on trial."

CHAPTER 17

June 15, 1905
New York City

It's been a year since the disaster. I float above the stone memorial, revolve around the statuary, appraising the assembled. I don't know any of these faces. These people are strangers to me. It seems that all those closest to the tragedy have either moved away, or they're already here. In here. With me. Or they've moved on. So many of the spirits whom I used to see in Middle Village, Queens, or in Manhattan, along the streets and avenues, above the parks and rooftops, most everywhere, are gone. But I remain. I don't know how to leave. There doesn't seem to be an exit from this place.

So much has happened. Kleindeutschland is no more. Only a few of the people I knew growing up there remain. Only the odd butcher and baker still linger. In the end, though no match was struck, and no fire burned on dry land, Van Schaick's fears had been warranted: Kleindeutschland was the secondary blaze.

Despite Miss Hall's confession at the inquest, and although eleven were found guilty—including Frank A. Barnaby and the other officers of the Knickerbocker Steamboat Company, as well as Captain Van Schaick and Inspector Lundberg—only Captain Van Schaick was convicted. He'll serve another eighteen months in prison before being pardoned by President Taft. Then he'll live out his days in seclusion, morose, misanthropic, replaying that voyage again and again in his head. In contrast, the board of the Knickerbocker Steamboat Company escaped with a nominal fine. A few dollars. A slap on the wrist, in the end.

Kleindeutschland may be gone, but some good did come out of the pain; they say flowers grow best in volcanic ash. Following the inquest, dozens and dozens of new government regulations were enacted, allegedly ensuring that no such event would transpire again. Perhaps with less frequency, fewer dead, but it will. If not in New York, then New Delhi or Rio, Chittagong or Negombo. It will.

My family moved to Germantown in Columbus, Ohio, where my father reopened his clock shop. It looks practically identical to the one in Kleindeutschland. He'll continue to fix clocks and watches until his eyes finally fail him, in seven more years. He'll die close to fifty from cancer, calling my name out, shouting it, and I'll be the only one there. My mother will never recover. Despite the support of my father and Helmuth, she will carry a piece of Nixie's christening gown to the grave. Threadbare and soiled, it will sit in her pocket as they shovel the earth on her head. And Helmuth. Helmuth will surprise everyone. He'll move to Los Angeles and become a pioneering director. He'll retire at sixty from the motion-picture industry to manage his orange groves, surrounded by his seven children and fourteen grandchildren . . . all of whom would never have been born if he had turned right instead of left on the promenade deck.

The Golden Rose is long gone. The Goldsteins moved to Yorkville on the Upper East Side, where Otto opened a tavern called Henry's. It's not nearly as successful as the Golden Rose, but at least he survived the debacle. His son, Bingham, returned to visit family in Germany soon after the tragedy and will never come back to New York. He'll be killed in a hole in Verdun, in 1916— when his lungs fill with mustard gas.

And the Brauers (henceforth the Boschs) moved to Missouri. Louisa and Dustin Bosch were married. It was only one month ago. One month and four days and six hours, three minutes. August Bosch (aka Arvin) will become incredibly wealthy, working as brewer, master brewer, and finally VP for a much larger brewery in St. Louis. Dustin also works at the brewery as an apprentice engineer. In a few years, he'll come up with the concept of putting caps on beer bottles. He, too, will grow rich, and fatter and slower, and eventually start losing his hair. In two years, Louisa will give birth to a beautiful, seven-pound, twelve-ounce girl, with corn-flower blue eyes, whom they'll call Mallory—after her aunt.

I revel in their happiness. I can feel it, and it warms me.

The events of that day have started to fade; they had a moderate half-life in the memory collective. Because of Germany's role in the Great War that followed, the *Slocum* disaster will soon be supplanted, pushed aside by other, more appropriate tragedies; after all, most of who burned or who drowned were from Germany.

Only a few still remember. Like me. Only a few still remain unresolved.

CHAPTER 18

Years Later
Long Island, New York

The spirit does not grow decrepit. There are no bones to age. But thoughts grow old and feeble. They wear away like Nixie's christening gown. How could they not? Once thought, perceived, ideas and feelings do not vanish. But they fade. Even mine. They crack and crumble over time. They grind. Like stones in the streambed of memory.

I am tired now. From time to time, I visit what was once my body. There is so little left. I have become a box of bones. From time to time, I visit Dustin and Louisa; I visit Mallory, my niece. But I grow bored of simply being a witness, an insubstantial spy. And there are times I see things that I shouldn't see.

I tell you this, but I do not seek your pity. When I think back upon my former self, I shudder at the things I let preoccupy me. I wasted so much energy. I squandered so much time. And cut short though my life was, since the *Slocum* I've had the opportunity to live innumerable lives—to feel how others feel, think their thoughts, fear their fears, dream their dreams. I used to walk the earth bereft of understanding, bankrupt of insight, shallow and vain. I was a ghost, a specter. In the end, it was only because I lost my life that I lived it.

Now I am ready. Only one thing remains. It's my fate. My last duty.

Mrs. Barnaby frets. It's Christmas and snow has been falling for a good seven hours. The roads on Long Island are slippery. The guests are beginning to show, mostly late. She attends them as they hand off their coats to the servants. She greets them and ushers them in.

The men are bedecked in tails and starched shirts, the women in gowns made of silk. There is champagne and oysters, water chestnuts in bacon, and caviar, smoked salmon, and shrimp. A fine string quartet plays Haydn with passion. There is dancing and light conversation. Then the guests take their seats in the grand banquet hall and prepare for their sumptuous dinner.

I watch them as they eat. I watch them as they chat and laugh and flirt and pander. I watch them as they lie and brag and brazenly manipulate. I see them as they are.

Barnaby sits at the head of the table. He has grown cadaverously thin and quite gray. He blows at his bisque. He pokes at his sturgeon. He stabs at his goose. But he rarely eats any longer. Nothing tastes good. And his stomach is delicate, fickle.

As soon as the supper is finished, he stands and urges his male friends to join him for billiards. They follow him out. They file down the hall. The billiard room sits by the library. As the men grab their cue sticks, Barnaby moves to the library to fetch his cigars and his cutter.

He opens the doors. He steps swiftly within. The room is quite dark—lit only by a fire burning wanly in the hearth—but he knows it so intimately that he navigates through the furniture by rote: past the club chairs; the ottoman; the dry bar and crystal; the hand-crafted screen from Siam. The humidor sits on the windowsill. He opens it deftly, removes some cigars. He stuffs them one by one in his coat.

The walls are covered with books, and he stares at them absently. He stares at their spines without thinking. He can hear the report of billiard balls striking, the crack, then the thud of rebounding. He turns. He looks up. And he stops.

He can see me descending; through the ceiling, and down, past the books and the paintings. He grows pale. He grows cold as I circle. *Crack, crack* go the billiard balls. *Crack.* And somebody laughs.

Today, I am dressed in bright white. My hair is on fire, and smoke wraps about me like the wings of a swan. My eyes and my eyelids—they sparkle and blaze. My mouth is as black as the grave.

Barnaby waits as I slip in beside him, as I snuggle and wind myself round. He is cold. He is so very cold. He grows old.

I draw his face close, put his chin on my shoulder.

He staggers and screams. He runs from the library, banging his shin on the ottoman. He stands in the doorway, his face white as snow. He shivers and quakes. And the gentlemen gather. "What's happened? What's wrong?" someone says. But they know. They've all heard the rumors. Mr. Barnaby's slipping. Since the inquest. How sad. Mr. Barnaby's sick, going mad.

Later that evening, after the guests have departed, as he lies in his bed with his wife, he turns from his book and confesses, "I saw her again, in the library. I saw the same girl."

Mrs. Barnaby wonders if she should pretend to be sleeping. And then says, "Sure you did, dear. I believe you. Go to sleep now." She gathers him close, puts his head on her shoulder. She rolls over and turns out the light

But I am his lover now, and he's mine. Dustin was just one kiss, long ago, on a floundering steamship. It's Barnaby I come home to each night.

Epilogue

It took Barnaby seventeen winters to die. He was the last of the board members, the last of his kind. Though younger, Lundberg had perished already, from syphilis, and Van Schaick from a broken heart. Only Miss Hall still survives them. She sits there alone in her rooms late at night, and remembers.

It's done. I can see that. It's over, and I've told you my story. The truth. My confession. There once was a steamship named the *General Slocum*. She sank, and I died.

Will you lead me? Will you open the door, please?

I am finished. Will you let me come in?